Scope

Mariya Taylor

ISBN-13: 978-1490469744
ISBN-10: 1490469745

DEDICATION

I would like to dedicate this book first and foremost to all of the amazing people who encouraged me to participate in NaNoWriMo 2012 and who supported me through the process: Todd, Cat, Jia, April, Chantelle, Steve and everyone on my FL and FB friends lists.

I would also like to dedicate this book to the people who inspired the characters: Todd Atkinson, Catherine Henstridge, Anna Ballard, John Taylor, Bonnie Murray and Tracey Taylor.

Last, but certainly not least, I want to give a final dedication to Todd. Not only did he provided the original concept of the book, he spent hours listening to me hash out character sketches and plot concepts, pushed me to write and edit when I would have much rather have been doing just about anything else, and who has shown me what true friendship and love are all about.

AUTHOR'S NOTE

I hope anyone reading this book will remember that this first edition printing is still in the midst of the editing process and will grant me the grace of being a flawed person with imperfect skills.

May you find the beauty within the broken, the hope within the hollow and the love within the lonely.

NOVEMBER 1

November 1, 2012. The day I had feared for the past three months was here.

I awoke slowly, in that lazy way you do when there are no alarms or obligations to tear you from the soft world of dreams and slam you into reality. My eyes fluttered open and I gave a soft sigh as I let the dream of being held in strong arms slowly drift away. The reality was that I was alone in a cold and empty bed on the day of my undoing.

It was a day of undeniable proof to myself and the rest of the world that I was a lonely, boring, spinster. I had accomplished almost nothing with my life and would inevitably die alone while the neighborhood cats I gave milk to ate my fetid corpse. It would probably take the young couple next door complaining to the landlord about the smell for my body to finally be found.

Okay, I admit, I was feeling a tad melodramatic and morbid this morning. It was my thirtieth birthday and I felt I had nothing to show for the past thirty years and I feared I would accomplish nothing more in the next thirty years.

My life up until this point had been mundane and uneventful. Yes, I had accomplished things like graduating high school, getting a job, losing my virginity, renting a condo and maintaining a good credit rating. I wasn't a complete disaster of a human being. But all of those things were…well…things. I hadn't accomplished any of the intangible things that society values so much. I was unmarried with no children and no prospects on either front. My love life had consisted of two serious boyfriends (both failed before the one year mark and neither had much passion) and a few horribly executed blind dates organized by my well-meaning, but overbearing, mother.

I had yet to meet a man I could really love, let alone want to have children with. But that seems to be the way our society measures a person's success in life - by their marital status, number of children and square feet of their house. By this standard I was a complete and utter failure.

Unfortunately this is also the standard with which my mother measures success. Therefore once a week at family dinner I endure a monologue about how my mother had been married and created life long before she reached my age. The key message being that I had better step up to the challenge before I was too old and saggy to attract a man.

My life revolved around my work and my hobbies. I excelled at my menial office job and then came home to write, read, listen to music and work on crafts. I was now thirty years old and I had spent the past ten years living the life of a retiree.

Don't get me wrong, overall I went about my days with a smile on my face feeling relatively content in my quiet little life. Yes, my mother knew just how to make me feel like a failure, and sometimes seeing couples or women with children would pull at my heart strings and make me wish for a life I had never even seen a glimpse of. But for the most part, I was content.

But I also knew that contentment would not last forever. I could not keep living my life this way. If I did, I would wake up in another 30 years and nothing would have changed and I would have grown to hate my life and myself.

For as much as I loved my writing and books and crafts, my tedious little job I was a superstar at and my cozy little condo…I knew in my heart that I wanted more. I wanted excitement and thrills. I wanted passion and heat. I wanted to experience the unexpected and unknown. I didn't want to just walk along the beach of life, skirting the tide to keep my feet dry. I wanted to run into the ocean, feel the waves beat against me, and dig my toes into the wet, thick muck at the bottom and immerse myself in life!

But these were just the hopes and dreams of a woman who had no idea how to live. I had felt this way my whole life, and yet here I was, living my quiet little life avoiding the tide. I didn't have the first clue how to even dip my pinkie toe in the water, let alone jump in!

However, I suspected I wouldn't find the answer to that question by lying in bed all day. Reluctantly I got up and went about the usual morning routine of starting the coffee maker, brushing my teeth, and sitting down with the morning paper.

I skimmed the headlines as I sipped my coffee and nibbled my bagel. I subscribed to the local paper more out of a sense of needing to encourage the local economy rather than a desire to follow the news. It was all so depressing. People being robbed, attacked, raped, and murdered. I always tried to find an article about something good that had happened. If I was lucky it happened once a week and I always knew it would be a good day when I stumbled upon one.

Today, it seemed, would be a good day after all! There was an article about a local man who had lived on the streets as a bum for 20 years before he decided he should get a job. He worked hard, built a life for himself and he just returned from a trip to Brazil to build homes for the poor. It was touching and heartwarming and made me think that it really is possible to turn your life around if you really want to.

If this man could give up drinking cold turkey and go from being a bum on the street to the savior of a family in a foreign country, then certainly I could make something of my life. The question was, what would I make of it?

This man was now being considered as an honorary deacon of a local church because he said it was the Word of God that spoke to him and told him to stop drinking, get a job and help people. Well, the Word of God certainly wasn't talking to me, and I was pretty sure I'd go deaf waiting for it to happen.

As a writer and artist I've struggled with a lack of inspiration for years, but I've found that when you let your mind go, let the pressure go, and simply BE that the inspiration tends to creep right up on you. So I flipped to the back of the paper and started working on the brain teasers to let my mind work and wander.

A half an hour later my coffee was cold, my bagel was crusty and I had finished every puzzle on the page and felt no closer to inspiration than when I started. Feeling my drive for change waning, I read my horoscope hoping it would cheer me up.

> *~ Make travel plans. The road ahead is full of surprises. Go out and enjoy them! ~*

I read it three times in a row. Every time I read it, it felt more right.

Travel somewhere. I could do that! One of my friends - in truth, really my only friend - lived in Texas and she had been saying for a couple years that I should come down and visit her. I had a little over a week off work for my birthday (taken with the expectation of mourning my pathetic excuse for a life) and I had money in savings.

Scope

It was time for a change and this would be my change! I would follow the advice of my horoscope and go on a trip!

I logged online and sure enough, Kass was on. We messaged back and forth for about an hour figuring out all the details. By the time noon rolled around I had my flight booked and I was making a packing list in my head.

That night as I folded and packed my clothes I considered my choice of action. I had never really paid much attention to horoscopes. My parents being very rational, scientific people, I was raised with the perception that it was all nonsense. Out of curiosity I did some research into my sign and found that for the most part I fit the typical Scorpio stereotype. The most common traits for Scorpio's are: determined, forceful, emotional, intuitive, powerful, passionate, exciting, magnetic, jealous, resentful, compulsive, obsessive and obstinate.

Either I was these things deep down inside or I aspired to be them. Though most people who knew me would say I was none of these things, another common trait of Scorpio's is to be secretive and mysterious, leaving people clueless as to whom they really are. That was me all right. Kass was the only person in this world who even had a tiny idea about who I really was, and we had only ever emailed and chatted online.

But all of that was about to change. In just a few days I would be flying to meet her face to face. I would be on an airplane for the first time. I would experience another city for the first time.

I fell asleep that night feeling excited, nervous, thrilled and terrified. This was the biggest leap I had ever taken. I always played everything safe, never acted on impulse and rarely took risks unless they were well calculated in my favor. If I was going to break the mold of my life this was certainly one way to do it. And all because I was seeking inspiration to change my life and read my horoscope out of desperation and boredom.

Perhaps there was something greater at work here. I'm not saying it was the Word of God by any stretch of the imagination. I'm not even sure if I believe in God as any religion describes Him. But maybe this was a little push from the universe. A sign that if left to my own devices I would spend the next thirty years as uneventfully as I had spent the last thirty years. Maybe my horoscope was leading me down a path I'd be too afraid to walk without a push and a shove. Maybe I should start paying more attention to my horoscopes. They certainly couldn't do much worse with my life than I had done on my own.

NOVEMBER 2

I woke up with the sun streaming through my window. Once again I awoke in an empty bed in an empty apartment, but this morning I didn't feel disheartened by that fact. Instead of focusing on being alone, all I could think about was the excitement of soon being in Dallas visiting with Kass and taking an active role in my own life for the first time.

I got up and started the coffee while my mind ran over possible things I might do or see on my trip. I sat down with the paper and considered the possibility of having a vacation fling. It's something you hear about all the time, "what happens in Vegas stays in Vegas" type things. I'd never traveled and my love life had completely relied on having met my two previous boyfriends online on gaming forums and spending a year or more chatting and gaming before meeting in person. I had no idea how normal people went out and met and started a fling, but maybe on this trip I would finally find out.

I couldn't contain my excitement and my mind kept wandering to all the what-if's that this adventure held. Kass had found me a great price on a last minute one-way ticket, thinking not only would it save me money but it left me free to leave whenever I wanted if it ended up being too much for me.

I couldn't help but think that I would have to fly back by the eleventh after using up my booked vacation time. That didn't seem like nearly enough time to explore and live and reinvent myself. I kept wishing I could have more time to get the most out of this opportunity.

No positive news articles in the paper today, so I skimmed through until I hit the puzzle page. My mind contemplated all the upcoming possibilities as I distractedly attempted to complete the crossword.

With all the puzzles done as best as I could I turned to my horoscope for the day, half hoping it would have a clear message for me.

~ You know what needs to be done in your life. Do it and don't worry if other people will approve or not ~

I got goose bumps as I read it. I had hoped for a clear message and I had gotten one. I had been thinking all morning about all the possibilities of this trip and wishing I had more time. I could easily have more time. Not including the time off I'd already booked for my birthday I still had over fifty holiday days saved up over the past twelve years I had worked for MT Pharmaceuticals. I took the required five days off a year, had only taken a handful of sick days, worked unpaid overtime, took on extra projects and never asked for anything. I had never pushed for a raise, gone after a promotion, asked for any special treatment. I didn't even ask for time off to attend my grandmother's funeral three years ago. I was the best employee they'd ever had and I knew it, and I knew my boss knew it too. She adored me for all of these reasons and for all of these reasons she owed me.

From some deep well within myself that I hadn't known existed, I summoned the courage to call her and ask for more time off.

"Good afternoon. MT Pharmaceuticals. Sheena Calloway speaking. How may I help you?"

"Hi, it's Melina."

"Oh hi! Happy birthday! How is your vacation going?

You're not missing us already are you?" I could hear the laughter in her voice. I knew she was mocking my habit of coming in on days off and weekends because I had nothing better to do. I had always tried to convince myself that the laughter in her voice was derived from a kind-hearted nature, but now I knew beyond any doubt that she was not the 'pal' she pretended to be. She had taken advantage of my dedication to my work for years and I couldn't let that happen any longer.

"My vacation is going well. That's what I called about actually. An opportunity has come up for me to visit a friend and I'd like to take it. I'd like to take another couple weeks off this month."

There was a pause on the other end of the line and I knew she was debating her options to determine which would make me come back to work sooner.

"You've already booked your seven days off and they have been approved. Now you're asking for more time off?"

"That's right. I have over fifty holiday days saved up so there's plenty available. No one else has time booked off this month and this is a great opportunity for me."

"Yes, you do have the time saved up, and no one else has time booked off, but this is highly unorthodox. Not to mention it's rude to spring so much time off on the department without any warning. I really don't think this would be a wise choice Melina. We really need you here and it's very selfish of you to not consider the impact to the team and to me here."

"Sheena, I have considered the impact to you and the team, and it is minimal. There will be a stack of work for me when I get back, but there would have been a stack no matter how long I took. And we both know I'll clean up the backlog in a few days."

"I just really don't think it's a good idea Melina. It's not that I don't want to give you this time off, but you don't just answer to me. A last minute request like this, and for so much more time, has to be submitted to the VP through HR. Do you really want them to get the wrong impression about you? I know what a hard worker you are, but a request like this makes you look like a slacker who is taking advantage of the company's generous holiday time policy."

I knew the company policies and I knew the request was within her realm of authority. She was talking in circles and trying to seem like my friend and play on my sense of guilt and obligation. It wouldn't work. Not this time.

"Sheena, I am requesting time off until November twenty sixth. If it is approved or not, I will be taking that time."

"Honestly Melina! I am shocked at your attitude! You know how lucky you are to have this job, how well this company treats you! I can't believe you would behave this way. If this is the stance you are going to take then I can't guarantee you'll have a job to come back to on the twenty sixth."

I was getting angry now. I was not about to give in to scare tactics. I took a deep breath and said calmly, "It would be an unfortunate loss for the company if I didn't have a job on the twenty sixth Sheena. However, with my knowledge and experience I could easily get a higher paying job at one of our competitors within minutes and we both know it. I'll see you on the twenty sixth."

I hung up before she could respond.

I could feel my heart pounding in my chest. I could hear the blood rushing through my ears. I choked back a lump in my throat and breathed deeply.

I had never felt so terrified…or so invincible. I had never stood up to anyone before in my life. I had always been too afraid to demand anything for myself, even to gently suggest anything for myself. Suddenly I felt strong, powerful and in control!

Was this how people who really lived their lives felt every day? It was intoxicating!

The cynic in me said these feeling wouldn't last and sooner rather than later I'd be back to my old, meek self. But something I hadn't known existed was stirring within me. It whispered to me that if I nurtured it, that it would grow and I would become strong, and that I could feel this way every day. That if I could take the risks, I could finally start really living my life.

The excitement of the upcoming trip combined with my emotional high from standing up for myself got me through the rest of the day floating on a cloud. I cleaned my entire condo from top to bottom, finished packing and gave myself a manicure and pedicure as a treat.

I knew tomorrow would hold bigger challenges than facing my boss and I would need all the energy and strength I could muster. I headed to bed early hoping for a good night's sleep, but all the wonderful 'what if's' kept flashing on the backs of my eyelids.

Finally I fell asleep and found myself dreaming of flying high above the clouds for the first time in my life, and I couldn't stop smiling.

NOVEMBER 3

The sound of a car horn tore me from my sleep and threw me into the reality of Saturday. I had moved out of my parents' house when I was twenty, and since then Saturday's had become a day to be dreaded.

Most people dreamed of Saturday to get through the week at work. I offered to work every Saturday I could. The first Saturday after I moved out my mother invited me over for dinner. I had gone back for a family dinner every Saturday night since then.

These were nights of mediocre food and the kind of dinner conversation that could turn a person to murder.

Don't get me wrong, I love my parents. They are my parents, I have to love them. I know that in their own confused way they mean well, but they have been pressuring me and criticizing me for as long as I can remember.

My father seems like the quintessential 'good guy' and to his credit, he sort of is. He is a good man with a kind word for everyone. He looks like a tall, lanky, balding, beardless Santa. He laughs loudly and readily and has a knack for putting people at ease.

Mother always joked that he should have been a sales man because he loves to talk, and for some reason people love to listen to him. Yet, for a man who always talks and feels like everyone's best friend, he manages to never let anyone get close. If you pay attention to him, he never talks about anything personal. He never lets you see even a hint of what makes him tick. Looking back, I don't think I have ever had a conversation with my father about anything more personal than the weather or their neighbors

Chihuahua making a mess on the lawn. Generally when we are alone together, we sit in awkward silence.

My mother, on the other hand, is a real piece of work. She fully admits that she married my father because he was dependable with a steady income and she belittles my dreams of marrying for love. She is constantly comparing me to her at my age and pointing out my lack of husband, child and social status. Once I turned twenty five she considered me an old maid and started buying me knitting needles and wool, though I have never knitted a thing in my life.

For as much as she demands her own way in all things, big and small, she has told me my whole life that "good girls do as they are told with a smile" and whenever I would even think of pushing back she seemed to know and would glare at me until I gave up, cowering.

The hardest thing to deal with when it comes to my mother is that no one else sees any of this. She looks like a leaner version of Edith Bunker and people assume she's just as sweet as that delightful fictional character. In public she will insult with a compliment, but most people don't catch on because she does it in a sugary sweet voice. The rest of it she holds in until you get home and then she will lecture for an hour or more about what an ungrateful child she has.

I spent the afternoon running around the house doing last minute preparations for the trip and trying to decide how I was going to break the news to my parents that I was taking this leap. I knew my father would smile and nod and not say a word. I also knew my mother would protest vehemently. I was terrified. Yes, I had stood up to my boss yesterday and it had felt amazing! But my mother was a whole other animal with a lifetime worth of fear and guilt behind her.

As I was getting changed to go over I was building up walls in my heart and mind as preparation and I realized that I had not yet read my horoscope. Yesterday it had given me the push I needed, perhaps the stars would help me out again today.

~ Stand up for yourself no matter how tough the opposition or how daunting the obstacles that stand in your way ~

Even though they were just words on paper written by a complete stranger and I still wasn't sure if I really believed there was any validity to the 'science' of horoscopes - I suddenly felt more confident about the impending dinner.

I rang the doorbell and stood on the front step with a smile on my face and happiness in my heart. I would not allow my mother to take this away from me or in any way diminish it.

She answered the door looking every inch a fifties housewife in her flowered dress, apron, heals and pearls. As soon as she saw the smile on my face, her own smile dropped into a frown of disdain, "What is wrong?" she asked in her stern, patronizing voice.

I smiled brighter and walked past her into the house, "Nothing is wrong mother. In fact, things are going splendidly. How have you been?" I let all my happiness and excitement show in my voice as I hung up my coat and beamed at her.

"I would be better if my daughter weren't acting like a fool. Have you been drinking young lady?"

I couldn't help it, I laughed out loud. No one laughs at mother. "No, I have not been drinking, I'm just happy. As for being a 'young lady', you may be ignoring the fact, but I did just turn thirty the other day. I don't think I am a young lady by anyone's standards anymore. And on that note, I am well over the legal drinking age anywhere in the world, so if I choose to drink that is my right and privilege and I don't have to answer to you or anyone else for making that choice."

I caught the look of stunned rage on her face before I turned and headed into the living room to greet father.

As usual my father was sitting in his recliner pretending to read the newspaper. I had learned at a young age that this was his 'me' time when he let his mind wander and ponder and imagine. He never actually read the newspaper, it was a prop to look like he was busy doing something socially acceptable so mother would leave him alone. I often imagined he spent this time picturing what his life would have been like if he had married a kind, sweet, loving woman instead of my mother.

I walked up and kissed him on the cheek - note that physical closeness, contact or intimacy of any kind never occurred in my family except at funerals - then plopped down on the couch smiling at him. The look on his face when he turned to me was something that should have been caught on camera. It was a look of happiness, surprise, love and tenderness. For the first time in my life I felt I was seeing my father's true face, and it was beautiful.

He leaned forward in his chair and put down his paper, "I heard what you said to your mother as you came in," he whispered in a conspiratorial tone, "I don't think anyone's ever spoken to her like that in her whole life! Did she collapse on the floor, burst into flames or just stand there dumbstruck?"

I laughed out loud, causing father to sit back in his chair out of fear that mother would hear my laugh, come in to see what the ruckus was and know we had been talking about her.

"It was mostly the dumbstruck."

There was a twinkle in his eye as he smiled wistfully, "I would have liked to have seen that."

"My ungrateful child and louse of a husband can come and eat now if they are done whispering about me in there!"

I don't think I had ever heard her sound so disapproving and cold. I repeated the words of my horoscope to myself over in my mind, then smiled warmly at my father, "Don't worry…I think you'll get to see it again soon…I have news."

I let the salad and soup course go by with a smile on my face and not a word spoken as my mother prattled on. I got to hear all about how her friend's daughters are married and giving them grand-babies and I'm a useless let down. Half way through the pork roast with mashed potatoes and asparagus, when she had her mouth full of food and therefore had stopped talking for a moment, I blurted out, "I've decided to take a trip to Texas to visit with Kass. I got a one way ticket and am not sure when I'll be coming back."

In a very uncharacteristic moment of unladylike behaviour; my mother spit out her mashed potatoes from shock. With mashed potatoes on her chin her mouth gaped at me, slowly opening and closing as she searched for words, giving her the appearance of a startled fish. My father had dropped his fork and was staring intently at my mother, trying his best to hide his grin.

Finally her words found her and she let loose in her strongest tone of matronly disapproval, "You are doing what!? Did you think to even consult your father and me about this cockamamie scheme of yours!? And who is this 'Kass' person? You know her from the internet, you don't know if she's even a real person! This is impulsive and dangerous and I do not approve! You cancel this hair-brained trip right now young lady! You come to your senses and stay put right here! Maybe take your time off work to do something productive, like try to meet a nice man, but don't you dare do something as ludicrous as abandon your father and I and run off to some desert where people eat hay and say "y'all" and practice incest! What kind of a man are you going to meet out there? One with webbed feet, a hairy back and nothing between his ears that's what!"

I didn't think it was possible, but I felt the smile on my face grow even wider.

"What are you smiling about? Stop smiling like that!" she had raised her voice to a shrieking level I'm surprised the human ear could still perceive.

I kept smiling and stood up, "Thank you for yet another delightful family dinner full of overcooked bland food, insults, condescension, belittlement and power trips. It's been swell, we'll have to do this again…never. I need to head home and finish packing. I fly out in the morning. I will text father and let him know when I have landed and once I know when I fly back home. It's time to make some changes in my life and this trip is the first one of them. Telling you that I am done with these asinine 'family dinners' between three people who might as well be strangers for all the love they share is another change. And standing up to you and letting you know that you may have held control over me for the past thirty years, but no more is another. Goodnight."

As I walked out I saw my father had tears in his eyes and a look of pride on his face. The only time I had ever seen so much emotion from him was when the Seahawks made it into the Super Bowl in 2006.

As I left I could hear my mother yelling and screaming for me to come back and face her and how dare I defy her. As I walked out of the house I felt as if my smile were about to dislocate my jaw. For the first time in my life felt that I was on equal footing with my mother and not just a bug under her shoe.

After I had gotten home I was so keyed up from the experience with my mother and so excited for the trip that I couldn't seem to slow down. I cleaned things that were already clean. I unpacked and re-packed my suitcases. I kept logging online to see if Kass was around, but she was off all night.

I tried reading. After reading the same page four times without any comprehension of what I had just read, I gave up.

I tried scrapbooking. An hour later I was sitting on the living room floor surrounded by cutouts from magazines with no pattern or similarities and no pages complete.

Finally, I tried writing. Even though I had always been too timid to speak my mind aloud, I had always found comfort, solace and strength in writing. No matter how bleak life seemed, pouring it out in words always seemed to help. I had been writing poetry since I was about fourteen years old and short stories since I was around seven.

When I was little I had dreamed of being an author. Walking into a bookstore and seeing my name on the shelves. Pouring my heart and soul into pages and having complete strangers pay to take them home and read them and treasure them. Getting fan mail from people saying they could relate to my words and appreciated them.

When I was thirteen I had bought myself a book on how to get published. My mother had found it, and that was the end of that dream. After hours of hearing about how writing didn't pay and no one would want to read anything I had written - I gave up. I stopped dreaming of becoming an author and found comfort in simply being a writer.

And now, in this high state of anticipation, excitement and awe at my own actions over the past couple of days, I sat and poured out a poem so full of hope and happiness that I could have sworn I almost heard the "click" of cosmic puzzle pieces finally falling into place.

Living Free
Coming to terms
With my painful past
Breaking free of the chains
Society has bound me with
Saying goodbye to negativity
Regardless of what face it wears
Seeking out new experiences
Instead of waiting
For life to happen to me
Finding courage and confidence
I never knew I was capable of
As I start living my life for myself

As soon as I had completed the poem I emailed it to Kass. I knew she would understand the huge significance of the poem and be as excited about it as I was. If I stopped to think about our friendship it struck me as incredibly strange, yet it had always felt right.

With the words written I suddenly felt exhausted. The clock blinked 3:08am at me as I climbed into bed. The alarm was set to go off in just three hours. Thankfully I fell asleep in minutes…with a smile on my face and hope in the future in my heart.

NOVEMBER 4

My flight was scheduled to depart the Helena airport at 6:10am and after stops in Salt Lake City and Albuquerque I was supposed to land in Dallas at 5:05pm. This meant that I had to be at the airport by around 5am. I have never been a fan of mornings. Coffee makes them bearable, but I have always done everything I can the night before to ensure I can sleep in as much as possible in the morning. So my alarm was set for 4am, giving me a half hour to get up, have a quick shower, brush my teeth and take a cab to the airport.

Unfortunately, when my alarm went off less than two short hours after I had finally fallen asleep I instinctively hit the snooze button…and then hit it again. At 5:33am I salt bolt upright in bed, fumbled for my cell phone, called a cab and started struggling to pull my clothes on.

I had to skip brushing my teeth and hair and instead popped a mint in my mouth and pulled my hair into a pony tail. I remembered at the last minute to grab the newspaper as I rushed out the door with my suitcases.

Between the flights and layover's it was scheduled to be nine hours and fifty five minutes. Not to mention the hour or so at the airport before the flight. A very long day started with a jolt of adrenaline and no toothpaste. This trip was not starting off on the right foot at all.

As the cab swerved and weaved to get me to the airport in time, I figured I would take a look at my horoscope and hoped it promised that this day would get better.

~ Look on the bright side. If you let your anxieties get to you things will go wrong. Your thoughts create your world ~

This was certainly fitting. From the moment I woke up I had been a ball of anxiety. Worried about having slept in, getting to the airport in time, getting onto the right flight, making all my connections, my flights all being on time, not getting lost in the airports, Kass being there when I arrive, my luggage being there when I arrive. There were so many things out of my control that could go vastly wrong.

I had never traveled outside of Montana before. The last time I was even outside of Helena was when I was fourteen and my Junior High took a field trip to the Little Bighorn Battlefield National Monument.

Up until this point I had been so focused on doing what needed to be done before I could leave and thinking about what might happen when I was there. I hadn't stopped to think at all about the process of getting from here to there. Now that I was in the thick of it I was wracked with anxiety.

I took a deep breath and reminded myself of my horoscope. I needed to look on the bright side. My thoughts create my world. So think positive and things will be positive.

I kept telling myself that the whole way to the airport.
As I waited in line to check in for my flight.
As I went through the intimidating airport security.
As I heard my flight being called for boarding and sprinted to the gate.
As I sat down in my seat and finally breathed a sigh of relief that I had made it onto the flight.

The first leg of the journey was uneventful. By the time I got off the plane in Salt Lake City I was dying for a coffee and so hungry I was sure the pilot could hear my stomach grumbling from the seventeenth row.

Thankfully there was a Starbucks in the airport, and I made my way there like I had some sort of homing beacon implanted in my brain. The boy at the till hardly looked old enough to work there and he smiled at me, showing adorable dimples, "Good morning and welcome to Starbucks. What can I get for you?"

"Venti peppermint mocha, skim, extra shot of espresso, no whip and a chicken and hummus bistro," I said, my voice completely monotone. It was the same thing I got every day for lunch at the Starbucks in my office building and the words poured out of my mouth automatically, like a robot. The boy took it in stride and kept smiling politely as he asked for my name and took my money. I left him all the change as thanks for putting up with my attitude and my horrible morning breath I was certain had wafted across the counter to him.

I wolfed down the food in no time and then savored the coffee sip by sip as I people watched. It was fun to imagine what had brought them here and where they were going. The two hour layover had passed before I knew it and I was on another plane.

Even though I had just consumed a decent amount of caffeine, I was asleep before we had left the ground.

In Albuquerque I consumed more coffee along with a bit of quiche as I people watched some more. Now and then I would have a hit of anxiety that I'd missed hearing my flight being called, but I kept repeating to myself that I needed to think positive and things would be positive. So far not a single thing had gone wrong so even if it wasn't helping, at least it wasn't hurting, and I certainly felt a lot better than I would if I had been wracked with anxiety the entire time.

My flight to Dallas left on time and even arrived five minutes early! As I emerged from the double doors I saw Kass waiting for me. She stood out in the crowd, as I knew she would. We had never met before, but we had seen plenty of pictures of each other. She was tall and slender while still being curvy and womanly. Her skin looked flawless thanks to her artfully applied makeup which looked like she was hardly wearing any at all. Her thick dark brown hair hung in casual tousled waves past her shoulders. Her warm brown eyes sparkled while she smiled her big smile that was even more captivating in person than it was in pictures.

Most people were wearing blue jeans and black jackets, but not Kass. Not only did she stand out because she looked like a model, but also because she dressed like one that had been splashed with color. Kass was a housewife so she didn't dress up to go to work, yet at 5pm on a Sunday night she was at the airport to pick me up wearing a rich teal colored sweater dress that cut off mid-thigh, a cute purple pea coat and a pair of black thigh high leather heeled boots.

As soon as she saw me she gave a little girl sequel and ran over to me, embracing me in a big hug. I had been feeling insecure about my messy, greasy hair, lack of makeup, black yoga pants, black turtleneck sweater, black suede ankle boots and black wool trench coat. But once she hugged me, suddenly none of that mattered. We were equals and I was accepted and welcomed and I felt so glad that I had taken this risk.

"I'm so happy to see you! How were your flights?! I got your poem this morning, it was wonderful! I am so happy that you're so excited about this trip! I'm so excited! I have been driving Liam crazy talking about nothing but you for the past couple days! Come on, you can tell me all about things while we go get your luggage!"

She was so bubbly and happy that I couldn't help but smile and feel bubbly and happy in response. I told her about how things went with my parents as we waited for my luggage. By the time I had caught her up on everything up until I had gotten off the plane; everyone from my flight had their luggage except me.

"Don't worry, it probably just got on the last cart. Let's head over to customer service, they'll sort it all out."

I was starting to worry, but she was so certain it would be okay that it eased my anxiety and I felt calm and confident that it would all be okay.

After a half hour waiting in line at customer service I didn't feel so certain.

"NEXT!" I walked up to the surly faced customer service employee and explained my situation. "Nothing's come in yet. Come back tomorrow and check. NEXT!"

I was furious that he hadn't even pretended to check his records. I was about to say something when Kass grabbed my arm and pulled me away, "Don't worry about it, let's just head home, have dinner and visit. You can have a bath, get a decent sleep and tomorrow we'll come back and your luggage will be here and it'll all be okay."

She smiled so big and bright and seemed so positive, and my mantra for the day was to think positive. I took a deep breath and reminded myself to think positive; that tomorrow my luggage would be here and it would be okay.

Driving to Kass's house from the airport I was struck by the fact that almost all the buildings - both residential and professional - were one story and made of brick. I had always had a soft spot for brick buildings and was captivated by them all.

By the time we were in Kass's neighborhood I was in shock and awe. I had known that her husband was very well off and successful and they had a nice home, but I had never seen a picture of it from the outside. Like all those around it, it was brick. A soft gray brick with darker gray shingles, white windows and white doors.

Unlike most of the houses I'd seen so far, it was also a two story. It was easily twice the size of my parents' house and well landscaped with lush grass and plenty of trees. At home we already had snow on the ground, but here things were still green and bright. Walking up the front path I saw bushes and flowers in a bed all along the front of the house. It seemed so perfect and lovely, like something from a movie instead of real life.

The inside of the house was no less amazing. The front entrance and hallways were all a soft sage green with pictures of Kass, Liam and friends and family sporadically hung all over the place. To the left was a large formal dining room done in dark reds with a big cherry wood table, chairs and china cabinets which housed real china.

"I'll save the grand tour for tomorrow, you must be beat! I'll show you your room and then we can have dinner!" her excitement never seemed to fade, she was remarkable.

My room was the biggest bedroom I'd ever seen and it had an actual en-suite bathroom and walk in closet. The whole thing was done in shades of cool aquamarine.

I had no luggage to put away so I put my carry-on bag on the desk and headed down into the kitchen.

With Kass's husband Liam working late and her brother Kail - who lived with them - at the university studying, it was just us girls. We had a lovely meal of pasta and salad and by eight I could hardly keep my eyes open.

I lay in the large, soft bed in the fanciest room I had ever been in and I felt completely thankful and grateful to have Kass in my life. For her friendship, kindness, acceptance and for opening her home to me like this. My positive attitude today had faltered for a moment at the airport from losing my luggage, but other than that I had enjoyed every moment of this incredible day of firsts.

As I drifted off to sleep my final thought was; I made it…I really am here! If I can do this, I can do anything!

NOVEMBER 5

For a moment I felt lost and confused. This wasn't my room. Where was I!?

Then as reality descended I remembered where I was and I smiled as I snuggled down under the thick comforter to savor my first morning of freedom. For the first time in my life I didn't have my parents or a boss to answer to. This day was one hundred percent mine. I could lie in this bed for the rest of the day, or I could go explore the world! The possibilities were endless and the choice was entirely mine.

As much as I loved sleep and lounging in bed, that was not what I had in mind for my first day of freedom. I jumped out of bed and headed into my own private bathroom to have a shower.

I hadn't seen much of the house last night, but what I had seen was beautiful and impressive. Each room had its own unique color scheme and feel to it. Some were bright and modern, some were darker and more traditional, yet somehow it all flowed and felt like it belonged together.

I was still in shock over my room. Not only was it bigger than any bedroom I had ever seen, but it had a walk-in closet and its own private bathroom. And this was a spare bedroom!

I had always known that Kass and her husband, Liam, were wealthy, but I had never imagined this! Kass had never made a big deal about their money. She mentioned it when she would offer to pay for me to visit, saying the cost was nothing, but I had always assumed that was an exaggeration. That's why I hadn't let her pay a cent for my flight here.

After my shower I slipped on the pair of black yoga pants and black t-shirt I had packed in my carry-on. Having never traveled before I had packed one day's worth of clothing, one nightshirt, my laptop, camera, toothbrush and a travel sized toothpaste in my carry-on. Now I was feeling pretty glad I had been paranoid.

I wasn't sure what the morning routine in this house was and it wasn't even eight am yet, so I turned on my laptop to kill some time before I ventured downstairs.

The first thing I did was go to the website for my local newspaper and check my horoscope:

~ The only thing that can hold you back is a negative attitude. Look on the bright side – and your day will be brighter too ~

It was pretty similar to yesterday's…did that mean something bad was going to happen today to test my positive attitude? I hoped not! But just in case, I would work hard to stay positive.

I checked my email - just spam. I checked my Facebook - I liked a status Kass had made last night about my being here, but other than that there was nothing new. Then I had nothing else to do, so I bravely headed downstairs.

It was simple to get from my room to the kitchen, just out the door, straight down the hallway, down the stairs and I was in the kitchen. That was the extent of my knowledge of the house aside from the formal dining room to the left of the entranceway and connecting to the kitchen. I was worried about waking someone up so I was being as quiet as possible as I crept down the stairs.

"Well good morning! You're up earlier than I thought you'd be. How'd you sleep?" Kass was sitting in the breakfast nook sipping coffee and reading the morning paper. She'd spoken in a normal voice so I guessed we didn't have to be worried about waking anyone up.

"I slept great! I thought I would have slept in later too, but I guess I just couldn't wait to start my first day here! Get my luggage and settle in properly and then who knows what!"

Kass smiled at me, "I can't wait either! Liam's already left for work and Kail's already left for school so it's just us girls till about 3 when Kail gets home. Why don't you have some breakfast and I'll get ready then we'll head over to the airport and get this day started?"

"Sounds like a fantastic plan!" I said as I poured myself a cup of coffee.

"Help yourself to anything in the pantry or fridge you'd like to eat and I'll be ready in about an hour," she said as she stood up from the table. I couldn't help but stare. Even in baggy fleece pajama pants and a ratty old tshirt with unbrushed hair in a messy pony tail and no makeup, she still looked gorgeous. She caught me staring and laughed, "I know, big shock compared to how I looked yesterday huh?"

I couldn't help it, I blushed, "Actually I was thinking you still look gorgeous. I wish I could look even half as pretty as you."

"Don't be silly! You are very pretty!"

"No, I'm not, but it's sweet of you to say."

At this point she took the coffee out of my hands and made me turn to face her, "This is why you aren't pretty. It's not about your hair, makeup, body or clothes. It's about your attitude. You think you aren't pretty so it's like you exude ugliness, and therefore you are ugly. You have a great body, sexy full lips, big inviting eyes, thick silky hair, what man wouldn't be attracted to you!? But then you take away from all of that by not playing up your assets and giving off this vibe of dejection. You need to get the attitude to go with what you've got and you need to show off your assets, not hide them!"

I felt like I'd just been smacked in the face by her words and I burst into tears.

Suddenly she went from being firm and hard to hugging me and stroking my hair, "It's okay, let it out," she whispered over and over as I cried against her shoulder. When I finally felt like I could breathe and form coherent words I pulled away from her and wiped the tears from my eyes.

"No one has ever said things like that to me before. All I ever heard was that I was too heavy and my eyes were too big and my body should be hidden and no one would be attracted to me. I've always hated my body and my eyes and tried to hide my body behind baggy dark clothes and my eyes behind thick bangs. I don't know how to be confident like you; I've spent my life hating myself."

She hugged me tightly, "I know exactly how you feel. Believe it or not, I was the same. I'd always been teased that I was too gangly, had a mouth as wide as The Joker and thanks to having braces for five years in junior high and high school, I was teased mercilessly about how no boy would kiss me or I'd eat his face and his hair would get stuck in my braces. But you know what? One day I met an amazing woman who told me I was beautiful and sexy and she helped me see it in myself and in time I started to believe it and exude it and that's when other people started seeing it too. Beauty is in the eye of the beholder, we all have our own ideas of what is beautiful, but it also comes from within. You have to believe you are beautiful, and then you are!"

"Thanks. I find it hard to believe you were ever anything but gorgeous, but I'll take your word for it," I said laughing, trying to deflect the conversation away from myself.

"Well thank you for the compliment…maybe one day you'll be telling some woman she's beautiful and she'll say the same to you. If I can help you see half in yourself what I see in you, you'll have the fella's lining up around the corner before you leave! Now, eat something and I'll get ready and then we'll head out. I have an idea!"

An hour and a half later we were at the airport again. Kass had worn a pair of jeans with a purple blouse that managed to hug her curves in all the right places and a pair of black healed ankle boots. How she wore heals so much was beyond me, I'd be falling all over the place.

It took a half hour of waiting in line to even get to speak to the customer service agent. Unlike yesterday, this time it was a young woman who actually seemed to enjoy her job. She listened to my story, took down my information, did some typing on her computer, frowned and headed into the back room.

Five minutes later she came back with a look on her face that said she was expecting a fight, "I'm sorry ma'am. It seems there was a mix-up last night. Your luggage was put with the connecting flight luggage headed for Florida. It arrived there at eleven last night. An agent there called the previously connected airports but the staff who took your complaint last night didn't log it properly, so your luggage has been returned to the address on the tag. I am so sorry."

I stood there for a moment in shock. All my clothes and toiletries and shoes and books and everything were back at home, and I was here with nothing but two days of clothing and pajamas. The girl behind the counter gave me a sympathetic look and suddenly I wanted to yell and cry at the same time. Before I could make a choice about which of the two I was going to do, Kass gave me a quick impulsive hug, "This is so perfect! It gives us the perfect excuse to do what I had planned, and now you can't argue with me about it! Let's go!"

Still shocked by the news, and confused by Kass's response I stumbled along behind her as she pulled my arm all the way back to her car.

"All my things…back home…what am I going to do?" I finally mumbled.

Kass quickly flashed me a smile as she drove, "You, my dear, aren't going to do anything! Today you will be my personal doll and you will try on whatever I tell you too and if I like it then I'll get it and you will have to wear it because you have no other clothes! And then we'll go to my salon and I'll have my guy cut your hair and my girl do your makeup and you'll have a complete makeover! I'm so excited!"

I went through the next six hours in a haze of stores, fabrics, driving and insecurity. I hadn't been shopping with anyone since I was thirteen and my mother said I was useless with no sense of style and refused to shop with me anymore. Since then I had bought my own clothes. Mostly baggy blacks, grays and dark blues to hide my body under.

Kass would let me try on anything I wanted, but I had to try on her suggestions and she had final say on all items purchased.

"You wouldn't let me pay for your flight at all and it was just your birthday. So consider this little shopping spree my birthday gift to you. If it helps, I'm having a great time!" she said when I insisted I should pay when we were at the first till.

She really was having a great day. She loved looking at clothes and trying things on. I had always hated shopping with a passion. It had always felt like a test that I inevitably failed. But, by the end of the day I found that I was having fun too. I was starting to see the cute bright clothes as something to consider and not something to fear, and I was actually having fun trying things on and modeling them for Kass.

As we walked into the hair salon at three that afternoon Kass said, "Once we're done here you will change into an outfit of my choice and we're going out for dinner so that I can prove a point. I can't wait to see the end result!" and she passed me off to a stylist as she ran back out to the car.

I was worried the stylist would do something horrible and drastic to my hair. Instead he cut about four inches off the length, making it sit two inches past my shoulders instead of halfway down my back. He lightened my bangs up a bit with face framing layers and showed me how to quickly add some big casual waves to my hair.

The makeup artist complimented me on my skin and lips and couldn't stop talking about my eyes. I had always hated my eyes. I had been teased my whole life about having cartoon character eyes or deer in the headlights eyes. No one had ever complimented me on them before. I couldn't stop blushing, which made it really hard for her to choose a shade of actual blush to apply.

When I was all done I walked to the front and found Kass holding a bag. She led me to the bathroom where she presented me with my outfit for the evening.

Kass was a tall and slender size 8 so it was easy for her to shop anywhere and wear anything. I, on the other hand, was a chunky size 16 so it wasn't quite as easy. But, we had managed to find me four pairs of pants, two pairs of jeans, three skirts, two dresses, twelve tops, three sets of pajamas, along with a new winter jacket, winter boots and a few pairs of dress shoes. Not to mention the incredibly embarrassing visit to Victoria's Secret.

I had always assumed I was too big to buy anything there. Turns out I fit their largest size in bras, panties and clothes, which was both a thrilling revelation which made me feel somehow more "normal" and also incredibly humiliating.

It was humiliating because I had never been fitted for a bra before. You stand there topless in front of a stranger and she measures you all over. I was horrified when Kass told me, but she laughed and encouraged me to do it. It turned out I'd been wearing a C44 bra for years when I was actually a D42. I was amazed at how big and perky my breasts looked when I had the proper bra on. Even I had to admit I looked sexy wearing the matching purple bra and panty set!

In the bathroom of the Salon Kass presented me with that very set (my personal favorite of the three bras and ten pairs of panties we had bought) as well as a pale blue dress we had bought that day. It had a bias cut hem so in the back it stopped at my knees but in the front at my mid-thigh - I had never shown so much leg before unless I was wearing a swim suit - and it was cut in a v neck with little cap sleeves and an empire waste. It showed off my very well accentuated breasts so much I feared they would fall out, but Kass assured me they wouldn't. She topped it off with a pair of cute strappy two inch heals we had bought. Kass had kept trying to make me try the crazy four or five inch ones, but when I finally tried a pair I almost fell. After that she regretfully agreed to a two inch heal maximum.

While we were out she had picked herself up an ankle length sweater dress with a scoop neck in a stripped blue, purple and green pattern. She kept her healed ankle boots and touched up her makeup and we were ready.

The restaurant she took me to was fancier than any place I had ever been to before. I felt like I was in a movie! There were crystal chandlers and guys with violins walking around playing and serenading people. It felt surreal!

I was so in awe of my surroundings I wasn't paying any attention to the people around us. Until Kass grabbed my hand and gave a gentle squeeze, "That table of attractive young men just checked you out!" she whispered as she slowly led me through the dining area.

Now that I was looking at the people and not the decor, I did notice a number of men glance and then look me up and down and keep looking. Part of me felt I should feel outraged that they would objectify me like that...but the majority of me was flattered by their attention and interest.

Our table seemed to be as far back in the restaurant as possible, but when we got there Liam and a young man I didn't know were already seated. Liam looked sharp with his blond hair perfectly styled and his grey suit fitting his tall toned body perfectly. His blue shirt and tie set off his bright blue eyes which sparkled and somehow eased the sharp, angular look of his face. Together he and Kass looked like two models at a photo shoot. Two such incredibly good looking people could only end up together.

They hugged and kissed hello and then Kass turned to the other man at the table, "Kail, this is my friend Melina. She's the one staying with us for a while. Be nice!"

He stood up and shook my hand, "Nice to meet you," he said politely before turning to Kass, "See, I can be nice!"

Aside from both their names starting with K and both being tall, dark haired and fair skinned I couldn't see much in common between Kass and Kail. He didn't speak at all during the meal unless he was asked a direct question, to which he seemed to strive to respond with as few words as possible. While Kass was well polished, Kail was haphazard. He was at this fancy restaurant wearing black slacks and a polo shirt. I suspected sneakers instead of dress shoes. He was taller than Kass and she was wearing heals, and his hair and beard gave the impression that he would fit in better at a biker bar than a classy place like this.

During the meal Kass told the guys about my mishap with my luggage and about our makeover day, "So boys, what do you think? I know neither of you saw Melina before, but what do you think of her now?"

Liam was kind and diplomatic, "You are lovely, my wife has excellent taste in all things fashionable and you look just darling."

Kail nodded and without looking me in the eye said, "I noticed her."

I felt disheartened by Kail's response, until Kass started laughing, "From him that's a rousing endorsement! He usually doesn't notice women at all. If I thought he noticed men at all I'd guess he was gay, but I suspect more asexual. Seems your makeover was successful enough to bring out a little bit of the hetero in my brother!" then she doubled over laughing and Liam told her she wasn't allowed any more wine.

I went to bed soon after we got back to the house. I laid there replaying the events of the day and feeling like a whole new person. I suddenly had a body to show off and be proud of that got the attention of men. I had walked in those heals and that dress and felt eyes on me, appreciating me, and I felt for the first time in my life that I was a desirable woman. It was incredibly empowering!

It was also a little frustrating having all those men looking at me, admiring me, possibly undressing me with their eyes; yet going to sleep in an empty bed. For as much as I had issues with my body, I was a sexual being and had needs. I had lost my virginity at the age of twenty three to my first boyfriend, Kent. I had never enjoyed sex with him or any of the other two guys I had dated, but I had been handling my sexual needs myself since I was fourteen.

Unfortunately the toys I had brought with me had ended up back at home in my suitcase. My own hands would have to do for now, but if this trip kept going this way I was going to have to explain my need to stop at an adult store to Kass soon.

NOVEMBER 6

Easing my physical needs the night before didn't help much. I dreamed all night about mouths and hands all over my body and woke up a quivering mess of desire. I lay in bed debating between trying to get myself off again or giving up and starting the day. Finally I decided to try again so that I could actually think and focus during the day.

An hour and a half later I had done the best I could to calm my desire under the circumstances and had just gotten out of the shower. It was a Tuesday morning around nine so I assumed Liam had left for work and Kail had left for school. Figuring it was just Kass and I in the house again, I thought it was safe to wear the sexier of the pajama's that Kass had bought yesterday.

She refused to let me buy anything in black aside from a couple pairs of pants, so even my pajamas were colorful. All three had various patterns of multicolored plaid. Today I went with the somewhat sexy flannel nightie. I know, flannel doesn't sound very sexy, but imagine a deep V neck with spaghetti straps and a hem that hardly covers my ass…but in blue and green plaid flannel. At this point it was about the sexiest thing I had ever owned! My boobs were hardly contained and I wore a pair of blue boy cut panties underneath since I felt certain my ass actually was hanging out.

I grabbed my laptop and headed down into the kitchen. The house was silent and empty. I assumed Kass was sleeping in to snore away the wine she'd had at dinner last night. I set my laptop up at the breakfast nook, started the coffee maker and was standing in the walk-in pantry debating between cereal or a bagel when I felt a big, strong hand on my shoulder give a slight squeeze of pressure and then a gentle nudge to the side.

I didn't scream, curse, or any of the typical responses to being touched by someone when you thought you were alone. Instead I gave a little "Eeep!" of shock before a small moan escaped my mouth from the pleasure of simple human contact.

I turned and found Kail standing behind me. His hair and beard were a little disheveled, his eyes looked groggy and he was topless. I glanced down and saw he was wearing pajama pants at least. I glanced back up and was face level with his collar bone. I could see the diamond of light hair on his chest that got lighter and lighter the closer it got to the waistband of his pajama pants. He wasn't an Adonis of masculinity exactly. No rippling biceps of a gym monkey. He was tall and lean and toned without being muscular or flabby.

Eventually I realized I had squealed, then moaned, then turned and proceeded to stare wordlessly at his chest…and that seemed a little rude. I finally made my mouth work and said in a strained voice, "Sorry. I thought you were at school and Liam was at work and Kass was sleeping. You startled me. I'll get out of your way," and side stepped around him and out of the pantry.

I poured myself a cup of coffee. Trying to redeem myself from my earlier rudeness, I called out "Coffee's ready, do you want me to pour you a cup?"

"Please," Kail's voice said from right behind me. I hadn't heard him leave the pantry and it made me jump and give another little "Eeep!" sound. I turned to face him and handed him the cup I had just poured, "You get this cup of coffee on the grounds that you agree to stop creeping up behind me like that. Deal?"

His serious and stoic face suddenly broke out in a grin and I caught my breath at how different he looked when he smiled, "I promise nothing," he said in his deep yet soft voice as he took the coffee from my hands and headed to the fridge.

His fingers had brushed mine as he reached for the cup and I felt my whole body shiver from just that little bit of contact. Clearly my efforts last night and again this morning had done very little to ease my desires if such little touches with a man who was essentially a stranger were affecting me this strongly.

Embarrassed by my reactions I hung my head in shame…only to see the massive amount of cleavage I was exposing looking up at me. I had been so distracted by Kail I had forgotten what I was wearing. Suddenly my face went red and I wanted to crawl into a hole and hide! I couldn't go and change now, it would be too obvious…but I couldn't stay here dressed like this and have coffee and breakfast with him.

Could I?

He hadn't seemed to notice my clothing - or lack thereof - nor be bothered by it. Maybe Kass had been right last night about him being gay or asexual. Maybe it would be okay. Maybe he didn't care at all.

I took a deep breath, poured myself a cup of coffee, decided on a bagel and sat down at the table with my laptop and began eating while I pulled up my horoscope for the day.

~ Expect the unexpected. Communication is key. Listen and speak with an open heart and it will open doors you can't even imagine ~

'Expect the unexpected' well maybe if I had read my horoscope before coming downstairs I wouldn't have been so surprised by Kail being home on a weekday! Lesson learned...read my scope before leaving my room!

Speaking of Kail...he was now sitting across from me sipping his coffee, eating a slice of toast and staring out the window behind me. Clearly my choice of pajamas didn't bother him or attract him since he was too busy looking outside into the backyard to even notice my cleavage. I felt better...and somehow insulted, all at the same time.

I mean, I had ogled him, why couldn't he ogle me back? Even just a little bit?

I laughed out loud at my own vanity, and he turned to look at me with a questioning look on his face. I blushed, smiled and said, "Nothing, ignore me," in a soft voice. He flashed a grin and said, "Not possible," and then he got up and headed back upstairs.

What had just happened!? The guy who last night I could have sworn was not at all my type was suddenly so yummy I couldn't stop staring at his chest and the briefest of touches made me quiver. And that same guy who last night complimented me, today seems not to notice me at all when I'm hardly covering anything, but then he says something cryptic about not being able to ignore me and then he walks away. I was so confused!

My head in my hands trying to make some sort of sense out of this, I didn't hear anything so when I felt yet another hand on my shoulder I let out an actual scream, "I told you to stop doing that!" I yelled as I spun around to give Kail a tongue lashing.

Instead I found Kass standing behind me wearing jeans and a pink tank top with her hair in a ponytail. This was the most casual I had seen her so far.

"Sorry, didn't mean to startle you, but there's no need to yell when someone is hung over…or get mad at them for doing something you told them not to do when you didn't tell them not to do anything. I need coffee," she reached past me and took my cup and downed it all. I couldn't help but smile. I had known and loved her for years online and meeting her in person had only strengthened my feelings of friendship and admiration for her. But this was a far more human side to her than I had ever seen before. It felt good to know that even the beautiful shiny people have bad days now and then.

She poured two fresh cups of coffee and sat down beside me, "So who did you think I was and what had you told me not to do?"

"Sorry. I had assumed Liam was at work and Kail was at school and you were sleeping in so I figured I had the place to myself. I was in the pantry and Kail came up behind me and scared me, then did it again just a couple minutes later at the coffee maker. It was embarrassing and awkward and I think you were wrong yesterday."

"Hmm…what was I wrong about?"

"Either you were wrong about me being pretty and sexy and attractive, or wrong about your brother being straight. He saw me in this and didn't even blink or even look!"

She smiled, "I certainly wasn't wrong about you being pretty and sexy…especially in that! If my brother was in the same room as you in that and he didn't stare slack-jawed at your boobs then he's got to be gay. I just wish he'd come out of the closet already and let the rest of us stop guessing!"

I laughed and felt better. Somehow Kass always knew just what to say to lighten any mood.

"So here's the scoop for today. Kail has Tuesday's and Thursday's without classes so sometimes he's here, sometimes he's not. I, however, have plans today. Before I knew you were coming I had agreed to help a friend out with a bake sale for her son's school. So I've got to leave right away and won't be back until sometime this afternoon. Will you be okay here?"

"Oh don't worry about me, I'll be just fine. It'll give me a chance to relax a little, maybe take a walk around the neighborhood," I said, meaning every work but deep down thinking that it would give me time to surf some porn and try to get myself off enough to not be a giant walking orgasm waiting to happen.

"Thanks. I feel bad, like I'm abandoning you or something. We have the big screen with satelite and Netflix and pay-per-view, feel free to watch anything you'd like. The drawer beside the sink has take-out menu's and we have accounts with all of them so you can order anything you'd like on us, and I'll be home as soon as possible. I really do need to run though. Have a good day sweetie!"

And just like that she was gone. She somehow always seemed to be in motion, even sitting still. I remained in awe of her constantly.

My breakfast done I gathered up my laptop and headed up to my room. At the top of the stairs I found Kail sitting on the couch in the sitting room at the landing. Our eyes met and I turned to rush down the hall in shame, until he called out to me.

"Wait a second…can we talk?"

Talk? Talking was communication and I was supposed to be open to communication today. I wanted to run and hide, but I made myself go over to the couch. I bent to put my laptop on the coffee table and when I looked over at Kail he was clearly staring at my boobs. I felt a thrill of accomplishment, pride and lust run through my body and had to clear my throat to mask the deep breath I took to calm myself down.

I sat in the chair to the left of the couch he was on and curled my legs underneath me to keep from flashing my panties at him.

"I didn't mean to eavesdrop, honest! Voices carry up the stairs really well and I heard you and Kass. I swear I am not gay. I understand why my sister thinks I might be, but I'm really not. And I'm sorry if I somehow offended you or made you think you were unattractive by not objectifying you. I thought I was being a gentleman and making you feel comfortable in our home by acting as if you were covered from head to toe. If it makes you feel better, it was a physical pain to not just stare at you…why is why I came up here."

I wasn't sure how to process this information or what to say in response. What I wanted to say was, 'thanks, it makes me feel better that you wanted to stare at my boobs, you can stare as much as you'd like. In fact, if you want I'll take off all my clothes and you do anything you'd like with them!' but that seemed incredibly inappropriate and like I was thinking with my crotch and not my mind…which I sort of was at this moment.

Instead I mumbled out, "Thanks. If it makes you feel better I felt like an idiot because I openly stared at your chest. So now we've both stared at each other's chests and we'll call it even. Ok?"

He flashed that grin again and it caught my breath in my throat and sent shivers down my spine. What was wrong with me!?

"I could argue that you got to see my chest bare and stare at it while yours is covered and I tried not to stare…but sure…we'll call it even."

Oh he was killing me! I felt the color rise in my cheeks and knew I was blushing furiously red, which just made me blush even more from embarrassment that I was blushing!"

He grinned wider, "Did you know that when you blush it's not only your cheeks that get red?"

I obviously gave him my best confused expression because he smiled and glanced at my cleavage. I looked down and saw that my chest had indeed flushed as well. I blushed harder and couldn't look up at him. I heard him chuckle in his deep, masculine way and say, "Don't be embarrassed, it's adorable." Then heard him get up and walk away. I didn't move a muscle until I heard his bedroom door close.

I spent the rest of the day avoiding Kail as much as possible. Part of me wanted to prance around in my bra and panties and see how long it took before one of us raped the other, but again, that seemed impolite.

Instead, I spent most of my time either in my room or on the patio reading or surfing the net. Our paths crossed a few times and I couldn't bring myself to look him in the eye. I kept my head down and responded to his few questions with nods, grunts and as few words as possible.

Finally Kass came home and I helped her make chicken, potatoes and fresh veggies for dinner. Since Liam had actually come home in time for dinner tonight, Kass suggested a board game with the four of us. We played a game of Risk. Kail won and I came in second with Kass losing and swearing up and down that Kail had cheated at board games her whole life because he always seemed to win. Then I said I was tired and wanted to head to bed early.

It was only ten, but I needed some privacy. I felt like my body was on fire and if I didn't do something about it soon it would swallow me whole.

I tried reading erotica, I tried watching porn, I tried fantasizing on my own. It didn't matter what I tried, I kept coming back to the visual of Kale standing there shirtless and the feeling of his hand on my shoulder. Once he came into my mind I always made myself stop. It felt wrong to get off to the image of my best friend's brother.

Eventually I fell asleep more sexually frustrated than I could remember having ever been.

NOVEMBER 7

It was another restless night dreaming of hands and mouths all over my body and constantly waking up in a feverish sweat. By eight I had given up all hope of sleep and I got out of bed and showered. My day had to start sometime and since I was neither sleeping in my bed, or doing anything else in it, I might as well get up and act like I wasn't about to explode with sexual tension.

This time I checked my scope before I left my room. It was as cryptic as ever.

> *~ Cast your fears aside and speak the bold truth today. The only things that can hold you back are self-doubt and silence ~*

Self-doubt and silence were my go-to ways to cope. Today felt like one of those days I want to hide all the time. But, I cast my fears aside and headed downstairs anyway.

Kass and Kail were sitting at the table eating breakfast in silence. As soon as I walked into the kitchen Kail picked up his unfinished bowl of cereal and went upstairs. Kass frowned at his back as he walked away, then turned and smiled brightly at me, "Good morning, how'd you sleep last night?"

"Not well. Need coffee." I said in a monotone voice of discontent.

"Awww, was the bed not comfortable enough? Were we too noisy? Anything I can do to help?"

She was being so sweet and thoughtful and caring and it made me want to scream, 'there's nothing you can do to help unless you can grow a penis and screw my brains out!'

but that seemed rude and unappreciative of all she had done for me. I took a deep breath and instead said, "The bed is great, you guys weren't noisy at all and there's nothing you can do to help. I've just been having dreams that make it hard to get a good night's rest that's all."

I sat down at the table next to her with my coffee in my hands and let out a small moan of pleasure as I took my first sip.

"Dreams huh? What kind of dreams?" she asked, her voice full of curiosity and a hint of teasing.

"Dreams. Just dreams. The kind that make you wake up three times an hour so you feel like crap in the morning," I said in my best 'don't poke the bear' voice.

"Oh those kinds of dreams. There's a cure for those kinds of dreams you know dear…it's called getting laid." This time her voice was full of teasing and I couldn't help but smile.

"Easier said than done. It's been about three years since I last got laid! In case you haven't caught on yet, I'm rather socially awkward and completely inept when it comes to flirting and dating and getting a guy into bed. If I can't do it at home where I feel safe, how the hell am I supposed to do it here where I feel like a tourist?"

"Well I see two options. One, you take matters into your own hands. Two, you go out on a date here! I know some nice guys, Liam works with a bunch of young eligible men. We can hook you up," I knew that tone in her voice…it was the same tone she had while she was plotting my makeover. I suspected she was already going through the list of men she knew trying to match me up.

"I've tried taking matters into my own hands, it's not helping. All my…um…tools of the trade got shipped back home in my luggage and my imagination keeps providing me with images that are disturbing so I don't get anywhere," my voice had turned whiny and I felt like crying from frustration. I sighed and plopped my head on Kass's shoulder and she stroked my hair gently, "There there dear, we'll figure something out," she said soothingly.

We sat there like that for a minute or two, my head on her shoulder and her stroking my hair, neither of us saying anything. It felt really good. Comforting, safe, warm and full of love. It felt the way I had always imagined a child would feel receiving comfort from their mother. It was a feeling I'd never had before.

The moment was broken when Kass tentatively said, "It's okay if it's too personal and you don't want to answer…but I'm curious what the disturbing images you've been having are."

I almost made up some lame fib about nightmares, but my scope had said to speak the bold truth. Kass had always been a very open, accepting person, so I took a deep breath and went for it.

"I don't want to upset you or gross you out or anything, but after you left yesterday, Kail and I had another run-in and he was cryptic, but I think he was trying to say he was attracted to me. This is the part that might gross you out…I'm attracted to him too. And last night when I would try it would start out fine but when I'd get close it'd change and I'd see him. And somehow getting off thinking about my best friend's brother seemed wrong so I kept stopping and then trying again and it kept happening so finally I gave up."

I was expecting anger at Kail for hitting on me, or disgust that someone would be attracted to her brother. What I wasn't expecting was laughter. It wasn't just a chuckle either; it was a big gulping belly laugh that lasted a couple minutes before she calmed down enough to talk.

"Sorry, I wasn't laughing at you. I was laughing at BOTH of you! Before you came down this morning Kail was in here and he asked how long you were staying and I said I didn't know, it was up to you. Then he asked if I'd be upset if something happened between you two and I told him that if you were both willing and happy then it had nothing to do with me. Then you came down and he ran away. Then you say this and I bet if he came down now you would run away too. Both of you are so adorably hopeless."

I could feel the confused frown on my face and when she saw it, she burst out laughing again.

"Sorry, sorry, it's just so cute! Tell you what, you leave it to me. I'll arrange a date for you two for tonight and we'll see how it goes. No pressure on either of you for anything, don't worry about me and PLEASE don't think about me while your together, that's just creepy," she headed for the stairs laughing to herself as I sat holding onto my coffee cup like a lifeline.

How had I gone from being sexually frustrated to having a date with the cause of that frustration in a matter of minutes? I felt like the rug had been pulled out from under my feet.

I heard Kass knock on Kail's door, heard mumbled voices then Kail yelling out, "Kass! What the hell!?"

I heard Kass laughing and more mumbled voices. Then a door closed and Kass came back downstairs with a big grin on her face, "He's in! Eat breakfast while I start plotting…I mean planning," then she bounded off to her bedroom giggling to herself.

What had I gotten myself into!?

Once Kail had left the house to go to class I felt better. While he was still in the house it was as if there wasn't enough air for both of us to breathe. Unfortunately, as soon as he left Kass went into high gear.

She had me put on a pair of her gym clothes (consisting of baggy sweat pants and one of Liam's old university tshirts) and dragged me out to a spa. She had me exfoliated, waxed places that made me cry, soaked in mud, peeled, massaged with hot oils and we both got new manicures and pedicures. Then she had my hair and makeup done and we headed home. Kass had a huge grin on her face and I felt exhausted.

"What's wrong sweetie? You should feel energized and psyched but you look like your about to pass out."

"How do you do all this stuff all the time? Letting so many strangers see you naked and touch you and do all that stuff to your body? It costs so much money and takes so much time and effort. It hardly seems worth it," I said, sounding tired and whiny, which was pretty much how I felt.

"I did all that stuff before I met Liam, though it cost less money and took even more time because I did it all myself. He'll tell you that the day he fell in love with me was the day he saw me without any makeup, my hair a mess from just waking up, my legs hairy from lack of waxing for about a month and I was wearing a pair of baggy, ratty sweat pants and a hoodie that was two sizes too big for me. We'd broken up a month before and I'd stopped caring about how I looked. He'd showed up at my apartment with a box of my stuff he'd collected. I invited him in and we talked. He says it felt like the first time he was seeing the real me. That until then he felt like I was a trophy girlfriend who looked and acted the way I thought I should, but not the way I really was. He says seeing me that way and having a real talk about how we felt showed him that there was more to me than looking pretty and - "

I interrupted and burst out, "Exactly! So why go to all this trouble!?"

"Because. I realized that I had been doing all of it to get guys' attention, but also for myself. Having my nails painted makes me feel pretty and more feminine, so I act more feminine and confident. Being pampered makes me feel special so I act like I deserve to be treated like I'm special. And yes, a lot of guys say they love their women natural, but they also like to know she can clean up and turn heads from time to time, it makes them feel proud to have her."

"But I'm going on a date with your brother. Are you saying you want your brother to have me?"

We both burst out laughing at the absurdity of that statement and then sat in silence, deep in thought, the rest of the ride home.

Six that night found me sitting at the dining room table wearing a pair of jeans, a teal tank top and a terrified expression. There was fine china laid out for two across from each other with candlelight for ambiance. In the oven was our meal of steak, potatoes and vegetables keeping warm. The fridge held a fruit and cheese tray for desert. Wine glasses with wine chilling on the table and the house was silent.

Kass had gone to pick Liam up from work and take him out for the evening so we would have the house to ourselves until eleven. I had no idea what she thought would happen that would need five hours. Dinner followed by awkwardness until we both hid in our respective rooms would take an hour max.

"Kass, you home?" Kail yelled as he came in through the garage.

"Kass and Liam are gone; it's just us. I'm in the dining room." I called out with only a slight quaver in my voice.

I heard him walk into the room behind me, but was too nervous to turn around and look at him. I sat perfectly still, like a hare who knows the wolf has sighted her.

I didn't hear him move, but suddenly his hands were on my shoulders and I wanted to melt from his touch, "Looks like my sister really outdid herself this time; candlelight and my favorite meal. Shall we dig in?"

We ate in awkward silence. The food was delicious, but I didn't know what to say to him. When we were done eating I started to clean up but Kail reached for my hand, "I know my sister and she will consider it an insult if we clean this up. She'll think it meant we weren't having a good time so we tried to kill time by cleaning. Why don't we go sit down in the living room?"

Without waiting for a response he took my hand and led me down the hall.

We sat on the couch next to each other in silence. After about a minute of silence Kail smiled, "Well this is a little awkward isn't it?"

I let out a sigh of relief that he felt it too, "Yes!"

"I know why it's awkward for me, why is it awkward for you?"

Speak the bold truth my scope had said. Okay…here goes! "Dates are always awkward for me. Talking to guys is always awkward for me. Why is it awkward for you?"

He looked up at me with surprise on his face, "Why is dating and talking to guys awkward for you?! I figured you went on dates all the time back home. I mean…look at you," he said sounding shocked.

I blushed at the compliment and looked down into my lap…or what would have been my lap if the push up bra and scoop neck tank top hadn't put my boobs on display blocking my view of my own lap.

"Well, I don't usually look like this. My luggage got rerouted so Kass took me shopping. Everything she made me buy shows more cleavage than anything I have back home. I usually dress much more modestly than this. Everything from my collarbone to my ankles covered in black or gray."

I glanced up and saw that now he was blushing and looking away, "I didn't mean your…uh…chest. I meant just look at you, all of you. If you were in one of my classes and came in every day wearing a burlap sack I'd still never get any work done. That's why it's awkward for me. I want to just stare at you all the time like a slack jawed idiot. But, you're my sisters friend and you're living in our house and I don't want to make you feel uncomfortable or stalked and I don't want to be the 'he's Kass's brother so I'll be nice and give him attention' pity date."

"Don't worry, this isn't a pity date. And the other morning I felt like I was making you uncomfortable in your own home by staring at your chest so I guess we're even on that front."

He wasn't saying anything. Nervously I looked up at him and found him just staring at me with a look on his face I couldn't quite explain. It reminded me of a small child afraid of being reprimanded by his parents.

We sat there, eyes locked for a moment before he said, "Not a pity date?" his voice was soft, almost a whisper. I simply nodded my head.

"You aren't creeped out when I stare at you?" his voice was even softer this time. I nodded my head no. Neither of us looked away, but I felt his hand move onto my knee. My body quivered in response but I forced myself to keep my eyes on his.

"You really want to be here, with me, right now?" he spoke so softly I could hardly hear him. I nodded my head yes and felt his hand on my knee give a gentle squeeze. I couldn't control it, this time my mouth opened and a smile sigh came out as my eyes fluttered.

When my eyes regained focus he was staring at me with a look of astonishment on his face, then the look turned to a grin of satisfaction and he leaned into me. His lips ever so softly brushed mine as his hand gave my knee another gentle squeeze.

What little control I had over my hormones was washed away in that moment. I moaned against his lips and deepened the kiss as my hand moved to the back of his neck, pulling him closer to me.

It felt like we sat on the couch kissing forever, but in reality it was probably only a few minutes. I admit, I have only kissed two other men in my life, but Kail blew them both out of the water. My entire body was throbbing with need and I thought if he didn't touch me soon I might explode.

That's when it happened. His hand, which had been rubbing and squeezing my knee, had been slowly moving higher and higher. In my overly aroused state I had been instinctively rocking my hips in small circles without realizing it. Suddenly his hand had reached the top of my thigh and slipped down between my legs and I pressed my hips forward. As soon as I felt his hand against my crotch my head fell back, my body arched against him and I moaned.

That seemed to set him off because his hand was suddenly in my hair, pulling my mouth back onto his, as his other hand repositioned me on the couch. He eased himself down and now I was lying on the couch with him on top of me.

Then suddenly we were both still. He lay on top of me with his head against my chest, both of us breathing heavily. After a moment he moved to sit up, "Well this is embarrassing," he said as he sat a full arm's length away from me.

I took a deep breath and sat up as well, "I'm sorry, it's okay, I'll pretend none of this ever happened," I said softly as I got up to head for the hallway trying not to cry.

"Wait, what?" he said, reaching out and grabbing my arm just before I was out of reach.

"You're embarrassed we made out. You didn't mean to, it's okay. I won't say anything to Kass and we'll pretend nothing happened," I said softly, unable to meet his eyes, afraid he'd see that it really wasn't okay.

He grabbed my other hand and stood up, holding both my hands in his and standing so close I could feel the heat radiating off his body. I wanted to swoon and cry at the same time.

"No. I'm not embarrassed we made out. I was the one who kissed you first, remember? I wanted to kiss you, to touch you so much. I'm not embarrassed that I finally did. I'm embarrassed about it being so…I don't know…animalistic," he was blushing now and it was so adorable.

I reached up and cupped his cheek with my hand, "You are sweet, but passion is a good thing."

He nodded his head in agreement, "Yes, passion is a good thing. What isn't good is acting like it's just a physical need that can be met with any willing partner. I don't do these kinds of things lightly. I don't even talk to girls lightly. There is a very valid reason why Kass suspected I was gay."

I smiled at that. I couldn't imagine anyone thinking that a man who could kiss a woman with such passion could possibly be gay.

"I don't do these things lightly either. You would be the third guy I have ever kissed. Both of those guys I chatted with online for months before meeting and we went out on a couple dates before I kissed them. This is whole new ground for me."

Knowing that seemed to ease some of the tension from him, his shoulders relaxed and he smiled slightly, "So what now?" he asked with his words as his eyes pleaded for more kissing and touching.

As much as my body was screaming at me to jump his bones, I knew it would be a bad idea. We hardly knew each other. As much as we might want to believe that right now it was more than just a physical need that could be met by anyone, we didn't know each other well enough for it to be much more than that.

"Well how about we call this date two. Date one would be the blind date kind of thing at dinner with Kass and Kail the other night. It was awkward and uncomfortable, but developed mutual attraction. This would be date two with a little more awkward and some physical closeness while we get to know each other more. What we've done is okay, but nothing more for now. And maybe we should do something with a little more talking and a little less touching for a while. Is that okay?"

He smiled, "That sounds like a good plan. Any thoughts on what you'd like to do?"

Now it was my turn to smile, "Not to display my dorkiness to much...but I think you can learn a lot about a person by how they play video games. What would you say to a little Mario Wii?"

After two hours of playing Wii together I had learned that he had a great laugh, was surprisingly goofy and lighthearted, yet very focused on the end goal. He wasn't distracted by all the little shiny things along the way, he was determined to reach the end and succeed.

It was getting late and we were both getting tired of the game. When we reached a chance to save I cleared my throat, "I have really enjoyed tonight, and I'm having fun…but it's also getting late. If we're up when Kass gets home it'll be the Spanish Inquisition and neither of us will get any sleep tonight. I think I'm going to head to bed."

As I stood up off the couch he jumped up beside me, "I'll walk you…home," he said with a goofy grin that made me laugh.

I was very self-conscious as I walked up the stairs in front of him. I felt like he was behind me staring at my bum and I kept wanting to pull my shirt down to hide it.

When I reached the door to my room I turned around to face him. He had done the creeping up on me thing and when I turned I practically bumped into him he was so close to me. I looked up at him and smiled and couldn't think of a single thing to say, so instead I put my hand up to his neck and pulled him down to me for a kiss.

It started slow and soft, but quickly grew to the passionate heights of our previous kiss. Part of me was so tempted to drag him into my room and have my way with him, but I knew tonight was not the night for that.

Eventually I reluctantly pulled away from the kiss and looked up at him wordlessly once more. After we had both gotten our breath back he whispered, "You are amazing. I wish…I wish a lot of things. But for now you should get some sleep. This was the best date I've ever had. I can't wait to see you in the morning."

I felt myself blush and turn my head away. I felt his fingers on my chin, turning my face up to meet his glance, "I meant it," he said before placing a gentle kiss on my forehead, "Goodnight," he whispered with his lips against my forehead. I was swooning inside and didn't trust myself to form words.

He ran his thumb across my lower lip, sending shivers down my spine, and then he turned and walked into his own room.

I stood in the hallway for a moment, lost in the sensations and emotions he had stirred inside me. When I closed the door and collapsed into the bed I felt like a giddy school girl. I wanted to giggle and sing and dance and prance through a field of wildflowers.

I was asleep in moments and that night my dreams weren't disturbing at all. They were of Kail's strong arms holding me and I slept like a baby.

NOVEMBER 8

Even though Kail and I had gone to our respective bedrooms before midnight and I was fast asleep before Kass and Liam got home, I managed to sleep in. It was just after ten when I woke up.

However, I did not wake up of my own free will. I was shockingly snapped out of dreamland by Kass jumping onto my bed next to me and shaking my shoulders, "I can't wait any more! Wake up! I need to know how it went!"

After groggily laughing and realizing what she meant, I sat up as she sat cross legged at the foot of the bed staring at me expectantly.

I didn't know where to start, so I took the coward's way out, "What did Kail say?"

"He didn't say anything! He left the house this morning before I got up and he hasn't replied to any of my texts!" she sounded so exasperated and looked so frustrated that I couldn't help but laugh.

"It's okay, calm down!" I said with a smile on my face as I patted her arm. She was adorable when she worked herself into a tizzy and for once I felt like the calm, confident one. It was a nice feeling.

She took a deep breath, and then said in a stern voice that brokered no refusal, "Spill!"

I opened my mouth to speak, then closed it, then said in a bad Spanish accent, "No, there is too much, I will sum up…Buttercup is marry Humperdink in little less than half an hour!"

I burst into laughter. Kass, however, did not even crack a smile. "Very funny. Now, out with it! I'm dying over here! Don't make me run you through like the six fingered man!"

I got my giggles under control and finally said, "Like Inego, I will sum up. We ate dinner in mostly awkward silence. It was delicious. We went into the living room and talked a bit. It went well. Turns out we're both actually interested in each other. We did make out a little bit, but agreed to take it no farther that night. Then we chatted and played some Wii and got to know each other more and then we went to our separate rooms."

She breathed a sigh of relief, "Oh thank goodness! When we got home and the dining room was a mess I thought it was a good sign. But then you were both in bed fast asleep and we got home a bit early so I was worried that was a bad sign. Then Kail was gone and he doesn't have class today so I was even more worried. And you weren't getting up to tell me how it went and I was freaking out!"

"Yes, I noticed the freaking out part," I said while trying to hold back another laugh.

"You mock me, but this is the lives of two people I care about here! I would be totally okay if you two didn't hit it off, but I was secretly hoping you would."

Impulsively I leaned over and gave her a big hug, "It went very well and I thank you for sticking your nose in, otherwise I suspect we would have spent my entire vacation lusting after each other while we avoided each other and nothing would have happened."

She made a face of disgust, "Don't get me wrong, I'm happy it went well and you both got a little kissy action because you both certainly needed it…but can you please not use the word 'lust' when referring to my baby brother?"

I laughed all the way to the bathroom

My scope that day read:

~ *All things are possible for you now. Above all, have the confidence to follow your heart and achieve your dreams* ~

I wasn't sure what that meant, since I already felt pretty confident and that I was following my heart. I suppose I should just keep doing what I was doing.

While Kass continued to obsess over the fact that Kail had woken up early and left the house on a day he had no classes, I was not worried. She felt that it was his way of avoiding dealing with me the day after our date. I, on the other hand, followed my scope's advice and remained confident. Last night went well and he seemed genuinely interested in me and seeing me again. When a worm of doubt would wiggle in my mind I would play back the night's events and I was confident and happy again.

We spent the rest of the morning cleaning up the dining room and kitchen, baking biscuits and gossiping about Kail. Kass kept telling me adorable and embarrassing stories about growing up together.

It seemed for every sweet story she told me (like when he was eight years old and found a neighborhood cat attacking a squirrel and he chased the cat away and nursed the squirrel back to health) she also told me an embarrassing one (like when he was seventeen and broke into their parents liquor cabinet and spent the next day throwing up rum and Cheetos). I felt like I was getting an idea of who he was and I loved every moment of it.

Kass and I were sitting in the dining room going through old family photo albums around two in the afternoon when Kail came home. Kass heard the door to the garage open and called out, "We're in here! Come look at this!"

Kail came in a moment later and as soon as he saw the photo albums his smile fell, "Why are you showing her those!?" he asked in a disappointed voice.

"Because I think she has a right to know what kind of guy she's dealing with," Kass said with laughter in her voice as she pointed to a picture of a teen aged Kail at a LAN party looking like he hadn't showered in days - and he probably hadn't.

He got a pained look on his face, "Don't you think I should let her find out what a dork I am in my own time instead of right off the bat before I've captivated her with my one or two positive qualities?"

Before the two could quibble any more I cut in, "Don't worry, I think it's adorable. If it makes you feel any better, there are no pictures of me at that age. I spent all my time in my room reading bad poetry and writing worse while avoiding the world," there was humor in my voice, but a part of me felt sad that my teen age years had consisted of so much solitude.

Kail smiled at me and Kass chuckled, "It's true. She's shown me some of those old poems and they were pretty 'dreary. But she's gotten really good with her writing. I've been telling her for years that she should publish some of her poems or short stories."

We both heard her, but our eyes were locked on each other and neither of us answered. After a minute of silence Kass stood up and said somewhat awkwardly, "Excuse me, I'm going to…um…go away now," and she left the room stifling laughter.

We stayed there looking at each other for a minute in silence before Kail sat down next to me. "So you spent your day hearing all the horror stories about what a loser I am eh?"

"Don't be mad at her. I think she was trying to show me a well-rounded image of you. She'd tell me something sweet and cute and then something silly or dorky. And don't worry about anything she's told me, my own life can be summed up pretty quickly - born, raised by an emotionally dead mother who hated me and a father who hated his life but acted like it was perfect and didn't get close to anyone. No friends, no social activities, no nothing. I grew up in isolation aside from classes, where I was singled out for being chubby and smart. Graduated high school, started working, still in the same job. My adult life consisted of two boyfriends, a couple bad dates thanks to my mother and really the only friend I've ever had is your sister. That's my pathetic little life in a nutshell. So don't rag on Kass for trying to show me that in some ways we're alike."

He smiled shyly at me, "I wouldn't say we're alike. You're amazing and I'm a schlub. But for some reason you agreed to spend time with me last night and I'm hoping you'll do the same tonight. Will you go out to dinner with me?" his voice got softer as he went on and I could tell he was afraid I would say no.

I reached out and touched his hand, "I'd love to," I said warmly. He looked up at me and his smile made his eyes gleam. It touched my heart and made it melt a little that he was so happy I'd agreed to have dinner with him. No one had ever been so happy to spend time with me.

"Okay, good. I need to go change. And don't get me wrong, you look smashing, but you might want to change into something a little less casual. I'll meet you down here in a half an hour?"

He was being vague, but I was pretty casual in a pair of yoga pants and a purple sweater. I had a moment of panic trying to think of what to wear. Then I heard Kass fumbling with dishes in the kitchen and I jumped up, "Sounds good, I'm just going to go let Kass know so she doesn't plan on us being here for dinner," then I ran into the kitchen.

I grabbed her arm and whispered, "Help!" into her ear as I dragged her upstairs.

She helped me do my hair and makeup and pick out clothes from the new wardrobe she'd purchased for me.

Just over a half hour later I walked into the downstairs living room to find Kail sitting on the edge of the couch looking nervous. He was wearing black slacks and a blue dress shirt which made his blue eyes seem even brighter. He stood up as I walked in and then he just stared at me.

I stood there for about a minute while he stared at me waiting to see if he would say or do anything. It was like he had been paused as he was about to say something. Finally I took a step forward and said softly, "Is this okay?"

It was as if my words shook him out of his daze and he grinned from ear to ear, "It's more than okay. You're lovely. Let's go!"

When Kass picked out the clothes I wasn't sure it was date material. The skirt hung to just below my knees and was plaid in shades of cream, beige and light brown. The top was a cream colored tank top with white lace along the neckline and sleeves and under the bust. I threw on my strappy heals and Kass had curled my hair in big waves and done simple makeup. I felt more like I was going to work than on a date, but Kail seemed to like it, so who was I to complain.

I threw on the new winter jacket Kass had gotten me - a cute teal pea coat - and off we went.

Dinner was at yet another nice restaurant, fancier than any place I'd ever been before coming to Texas, but not on quite the same level as the place we'd been the other night with Kass and Liam.

After having salad, soup, pasta and sharing a slice of cheesecake we were both stuffed. We had spent the whole meal talking about our childhoods and his school and my work. We talked about our hobbies - my writing and his love of video games and working on developing his own - and that set off a conversation about dreams.

"I've always loved playing video games. So for me creating worlds and characters and plots just came naturally. I'd play a game and starting thinking about all the things I'd add if I had the power to make one of my own. I've teamed up with some friends of mine who are developers and we're actually working on one right now. My degree in business and finance will come in handy since I should be done school by the time the game is done. We're going to start our own business and market it and if it goes well we're hoping to make a living off doing this. What about you? What's your dream for the future?"

I suddenly felt like crying, "I don't really have one," I said softly, trying to hold back the tears.

"What do you mean you don't have one? You don't have any dreams, goals, aspirations for the future?"

I shook my head no and looked down into my lap so he wouldn't see the sadness in my eyes, "I was raised being told how the only dream a woman should have was marriage and motherhood. Since I was neither married nor a mother by the time I was in my early twenties I've been told I'm a failure. I've never had dreams of my own, only the ones my mother put there. I've failed at those so finding dreams of my own seems futile since I'll probably just fail at those too," by the time I'd reached the end of my sad little monologue I had tears rolling down my face.

Kail stood up and took my hand, "Come with me," he said in a stern voice that almost sounded angry. I was afraid to look into his face because then he'd see my own. I kept my head down as I stood up. He led me away from the table and when I tried to protest that we hadn't paid the bill he simply said, "It's taken care of," in that stern, angry voice and kept pulling me in a winding path through the tables.

I hadn't realized when we had arrived that the restaurant was attached to a hotel. Kail was now leading me through the lobby of the hotel, into an elevator, down another hallway and into a hotel room.

He closed the door behind us, sat me down on the edge of the bed, stood in front of me, put his hand under my chin and forced me to look up at him. He did look angry and I felt a small jolt of fear. Yes, he was Kass's brother, but I didn't actually know him. Here I was alone in a hotel room with him and he was angry. I didn't think he was capable of being violent towards me, but how could I really know? I instinctively jerked my face back from his touch and cowered away from him.

Instantly his face softened, "I'm sorry. I got so angry when you said that about your mother and dreams, but I'm not angry with you. It's true that right now I feel like I could punch someone in the face, but I would never, ever, touch you in anger," he slowly put his hand out and when I didn't flinch or pull away he stroked my cheek gently.

"I know that Kass and I were pretty lucky when it comes to our parents. They raised us to believe we could do whatever we wanted. When I was six and I told my dad I wanted to be a space cowboy he went out and bought me cowboy boots and toy ray gun. They encouraged us to find things we were passionate about and to pursue them. The fact that your mother brainwashed you into believing the only dream you could have was to be a wife and a mother is so destructive. Then for her to reinforce that you must be a failure because you hadn't achieved what she wanted according to her time line. It just makes my blood boil!" his fists clenched at his sides and then he knelt down on the ground in front of me.

He took hold of my hands and looked into my eyes, "You are smart and talented and amazing. You can do anything you want in life. You can be a writer or a wife or a mother or a space cowboy! You need to find what makes you happy in this world and go after it and don't stop trying until you have achieved it!"

The tears were now streaming down my cheeks as I looked into Kail's bright blue eyes, so full of honesty and fervor.

He truly believed what he was saying. It shattered everything I had ever thought or believed about myself, my abilities and my future. His belief was so strong that I couldn't simply brush it aside. It awoke something in me and a small voice in my head screamed through the darkness that he was right.

My tears had streamed down my cheeks to my chin to drip down onto my chest. Kail leaned forward and softly and chastely kissed my lips once, then lowered his head to kiss the tears off my chin, then off my chest.

Unlike last night, this time was slow and tender. We both took our time with every touch, kiss and caress.

Don't get me wrong, I'm not saying there was no passion or heat, but it wasn't frantic and needy. We both seemed to want to savor every moment.

We took our time exploring each other. I had always been self-conscious about my body and therefore had only ever had sex with the lights off or with candlelight. Yet with Kail I felt no hesitation to take my clothes off in the bright lights of the hotel room.

Unlike the other two men who had seen me naked, he didn't immediately maul my breasts. He took in all of me with his eyes and the first thing he touched was my waist as he pulled me close to him for a kiss.

It was hours later when we lay cuddled next to each other, both completely satisfied. I had my head resting on his shoulder in the crook of his arm. He was stroking the back of my neck. I had never felt so content or happy in my life.

"You are magnificent," Kail said as he kissed my forehead. I snuggled down into him and sighed.

"Don't hide, I'm telling the truth," he said in a stern voice. I looked up at him and smiled before kissing him slowly and deeply.

"I know you mean it and believe it. It's just going to take time for me to undo all the conditioning I've had my whole life that I'm unattractive and unskilled and nobody would ever want me," I said softly, resisting the urge to cry.

He stroked my hair and kissed my forehead again, "I do mean it. And hopefully one day you will believe it."

For the first time I was laying in the arms of a man who genuinely wanted to be with me, who believed in me and who made me feel good about myself. And he was the brother of my best friend. A week ago I would have said this was not possible. Yet here I was. If I could make it here, maybe it would be okay to have a dream. If I could accomplish this, I could accomplish so much more.

NOVEMBER 9

When I woke up I thought I was dreaming. Kail was lying next to me, spooning me from behind. I felt safe, warm and happy. It must be a dream.

I literally pinched my arm before I allowed myself to smile and relish the simple pleasure of the moment. I glanced at the clock; it was eight in the morning.

I sat up with a start and shook Kail awake, "We need to go. Kass doesn't know where we are, she'll be worried sick!" I was about to jump out of bed when Kail wrapped his arm around my waist and pulled me back to him. He nuzzled my neck and whispered, "She knows where we are. I don't have class until the afternoon. Don't you dare get out of this bed yet."

I sighed contentedly as I curled up against him again.

We both fell back asleep for another hour or so before our growling stomachs urged us to have breakfast. We ordered room service and sat on the bed, eating off shared plates of bacon, pancakes and fruit.

"So how does Kass know where we are?" I asked as I savored the sweet mango.

"I left her a note," he said as he munched into a crispy slice of bacon.

"You really planned this out didn't you?" I said with a hint of teasing in my voice.

"You bet. I wasn't leaving anything to chance. I knew if her and Liam were in the house it'd be too weird for us to be physical so I got a hotel room in case the opportunity came up. While you were sleeping yesterday morning I snuck into your room and grabbed you a change of clothes which I planned to put back last night if the date didn't end up here. I made the reservation at the hotel and left a note for Kass telling her that if the date did not go well we'd be home sometime that night. If it went well I'd drop you off on my way to class today."

I was touched. It was the most romantic thing anyone had ever done for me. I leaned forward over the breakfast tray and kissed him softly and whispered, "Thank you," against his lips.

We made love once more before sharing a shower and getting dressed. As we sat in the car on the way to the house I couldn't help but think that it all felt surreal. It was like something you would see in a movie, not something that real guys did. And if a real guy was ever going to be so sweet, thoughtful and romantic it felt so wrong that he would be that way with me. It was blowing my mind!

We got to the house and I leaned over to kiss him. He froze under my lips and I pulled away, "What's wrong? Is it me?" I asked, feeling like suddenly the other shoe was dropping and he would say it had all been a mistake.

He frowned at me, "No, it's not you," the tone in his voice was dripping with disdain. I gave him a confused expression and he sighed, "My sister is sitting on the front step watching us. I've never kissed a girl in front of my sister before. It feels weird," he sounded so unsure of himself all of a sudden.

"You are both adults. You've seen her and Liam kiss I'm sure. She's not my sister and I don't care if she sees me kissing a guy and I want to kiss you so suck it up and pucker up!" I leaned forward and kissed him long, deep and hard. At first he was stiff and reluctant, but it only took a moment before he'd forgotten all about his sister watching and was kissing me back passionately.

Finally I broke the kiss, "See, that wasn't so bad," I said cheerfully. He frowned at me for a second before a smile won over. I gave him a quick peck on the lips, "Now go learn something!" I said before I hopped out of the car.

I walked up the front step towards Kass as I heard Kail drive away. She was sitting there in sweat pants and her winter coat and boots holding a cup of coffee. No makeup and her hair a mess. I could tell she hadn't slept well.

"Good morning sunshine!" I said cheerfully as I sat down on the step next to her and put my arm around her shoulder.

"Don't 'sunshine' me missy! I'm starting to wonder if you and my brother aren't plotting to give me a heart attack! I was up half the night wondering how it was going. I kept thinking you weren't coming home so it must be going well. That made me think you two were probably doing things a sister would rather not know about. That kept making me go into the kitchen and eat more chocolate cake."

I hugged her tightly, "It was amazingly wonderful and I am blissfully happy and I won't tell you any details so you can stop binge eating. Let's go inside!"

I stood up and walked in knowing she would be right behind me.

"Oh no you don't! I need details! I can't even grasp the concept that my brother spent the night with a girl, and you show up all smiles and chipper. It's making my brain hurt! All these years I thought I knew him and now he's this totally different guy. I can't wrap my head around it. You need to help me fill in the blanks," she said as she chased me into the house and down the hall towards the stairs.

"I will tell you something…but first I need to check my scope. You refill your cup and go sit down. I'll be back in a second," I said as I dashed upstairs.

I threw my clothes from the night before in the hamper as I booted up my laptop. Part of me wanted to tell Kass everything. Part of me wanted to tell her as little as possible. As my friend I wanted to gush and give details. As Kail's sister I wanted to leave how much she knew up to him. It was a complex situation and one I was not at all suited to maneuver on my own. I hoped my scope would give me some direction.

~ You have learned to put the past behind you and focus on the future. Now it's time to teach other's to do the same. Each day can be a new beginning ~

Well that certainly seemed clear enough. I walked into the downstairs living room to find Kass sitting on the edge of the couch looking nervous. Exactly as Kail had been the night before. Really, the two of them were more alike than either of them seemed to realize. It made me smile.

"Sure, first you gallivant off all night leaving me worried sick and driving myself mad. Then you show up all rainbows and sunshine bursting out of your behind. Being all cryptic and running upstairs, leaving me down here on pins and needles! Now you come down grinning and smiling like the cat that ate the canary. I'm going mad here woman. Mad I say!"

I burst out laughing as I sat down next to her and hugged her tightly.

"You, my dear, are the best friend a girl could ask for. You are sweet, caring, supportive, understanding, funny and thoughtful," I said as I hugged her.

She fought free of my hug and said in a tone of desperation, "Yes, that's very sweet of you, and I feel the same. But we aren't here to talk about me. We are here to talk about my schlub of a brother and how he treated you."

"And that's exactly what I was smiling about when I came in the room. You were sitting there just as he had been yesterday when I came down for our date. You two are much more alike than you think."

She pulled away even farther, "I beg your pardon! I am nothing like my brother. He floats through life without any direction, goals, ambition or drive. He's never shown affection for anyone or anything before now. He was never affectionate with our parents or me, though the rest of us are all very affectionate people. He sullenly agreed to go out with girls I'd set him up with but they always said he spent the dates sitting there in silence staring awkwardly into the distance. He's never dated anyone of his own free will before. He has no plans for when he's done school; he's just coasting by being naturally smart enough to pass his classes without much effort and spends all his time playing his damn video games. How the hell am I like him!?"

I fought to keep the smile off my face because it was clear that right now it would offend her. "I admit I have no siblings so I'm only guessing here…but I think your vision of him is a little colored by the fact that he is your brother.

Did you know that he is working to develop his own video game, with plans of starting his own business to market and sell it? That his dream is to build this up into a legitimate business?"

That gave her pause and she shook her head no.

"Did you know that the reason the dates you set him up on went so badly was because he thought you and your friends felt sorry for him being a lonely loser so they were simply pity dates? He never once thought any of the girls were at all interested in him and were just going out with him as a favor to you."

"No, I -"

I put my hand up and cut her off, "Did you know that he considers himself lucky to have had the upbringing he did with you and your parents? That while he may not have seemed affectionate or appreciative, that he clearly loves your parents and you very much and is very grateful for all of you?"

Now she looked like she was about to cry as she shook her head no once more.

"Did you know that he feels like he's older than you but you've never needed him to take care of you, instead you have always taken care of him and he doesn't know how to deal with that because he feels like he has no place in your life?"

This time I saw a tear roll down her cheek. I wiped it away and said softly, "You both have a lifetime's worth of memories and perceptions that cloud how you see each other. Coming from the outside without all the history blocking my vision, I see two of the most amazing people

I have ever met. You are both caring, supportive, kind and genuine and I feel so lucky and blessed to know even one of you. That fact that you two are sort of a two for one deal just blows my mind a little bit."

I don't know what sort of a reaction I was expecting, but when she lunged at me and gave me a giant bear hug I was completely taken by surprise.

"Last night I kept thinking that he better treat you well and be good to you. I kept thinking he didn't deserve you and that it would be all my fault when you came home upset. I am so happy it went well! I do love my brother, I just don't understand him. Now I'm thinking maybe I've never known him. Then you come here and suddenly he's a whole other person and you're changing so much so quickly and I just feel so happy for you both and so honored to be a part of all of it!"

We hugged and talked more about Kass's views on Kail and her perspective on their childhood. I was formulating a plan for once Kail got home from class. I would follow my scope's advice and be the catalyst for change in how these two viewed their shared past and the future.

Kass and I were in the dining room going through old photo albums again when Kail got home. This time I was the one to call out to him, "We're in the dining room. Can you come here please?"

He came in and stood behind my chair with his hands on my shoulders, "This again? Really Kass! Hasn't the poor girl had enough?"

I tilted my head backwards to look up at him, "It was my idea. I want to talk to you both. Join us?"

I could tell he was about to say no so I threw in a, "please?" with a bit of a pout and he gave in, sitting next to me.

"Kass and I had a big talk when I got home today and I realized that you two are a lot alike. I don't have siblings so I'm not completely sure how these things usually work…but I don't think having skewed views of each other is a healthy thing. So, I'm going to say a little about you both and then leave you two alone to discuss. Ready?"

Kass nodded her head yes. Kail sat motionless. I reached for his hand and gave it a light squeeze. Finally he nodded his head yes.

"I know that Kass can come off like a vapid socialite at times. She is very concerned with how she looks and how people perceive her. I also know that Kail can come off as not caring about anyone or anything or their views about him. Both of you come across this way for the same reason. You both know you are amazing deep down, but you both have had experiences in life where people have made you feel you are somehow less. Kass combats this by trying to show the world, and herself, that she is worthy. Kail combats this by showing the world that he doesn't care what they think."

Both of them sat there staring at me. I wasn't sure if any of this was getting through, but I pushed on. I turned to Kail, "Kass can come off as being a nosy busy body who intrudes into your personal life without permission. Really, she worries about you. She loves you and wants you to be happy and feel fulfilled in life. But, you don't let her in enough for her to know what it is that makes you happy or fulfilled. So she's left making uneducated guesses and trying to find ways to connect with you and failing."

I turned to Kass, "And Kail comes off as being unambitious, lazy and coasting through life. Really he's working very hard towards a goal, but he's afraid to share it with people in case it doesn't succeed. He wants you to be proud of him so he doesn't want to risk telling you about things unless he knows they are guarantees."

They were both still giving me blank stares. I was getting nervous that this would fail and they would both hate me, but I pushed on. "You are both amazing people who I feel blessed to know. But you both see each other through all of these memories," I waved my hand at the photo albums. "I want you both to go into the living room and talk. Don't talk about the past. Don't talk about your childhoods or things you have been through. I want you both to talk about your futures. What it is you both want to have happen tomorrow, a week from now, a month, a year, ten years from now."

They both looked at me with apprehension and a touch of fear in their eyes. "Go! Now!" I said in my most stern voice as I waved my hands at both of them in a shooing motion.

I tidied up the albums in the dining room and could hear only silence. In time I heard voices, soft and tentative. I smiled to myself as I headed up to my room.

My clock read two in the morning when I woke up. I had felt the bed move. I turned around and saw Kail in his boxers climbing into my bed.

I scooted over to make room for him and we naturally curled up next to each other. "How did it go?" I asked in a groggy, sleepy voice.

"It started out rocky, but we ended up going forever. We just finished actually. It was pretty amazing in the end. Thank you. You are a remarkable woman," he said as he spooned me from behind and kissed the back of my neck.

I sighed contentedly as I wiggled against him to get closer, "I'm glad it worked out well. I was scared for a bit there that you would both hate me."

I felt his body respond to having me pressed against him and he whispered, "I could never hate you," as his arms held me tight.

We both struggled to be silent as our bodies moved together in the dark. We didn't need light, we made our own fire.

NOVEMBER 10

I had never lived with any of my ex-boyfriends and usually they left in the middle of the night after we had been intimate. Only on a few rare occasions had I ever woken up in bed with a man.

Slowly waking up wrapped in Kail's arms felt like the best place in the world I could possibly be. I snuggled into him and didn't ever want to get out of bed.

We were still spooning and when I snuggled in; he woke up a little bit. Then a bit more. Soon I couldn't tell if he was still dreaming or not, but it was clear that his body was awake.

"Kail?" I whispered softly.

He pressed against me harder as he made a soft "Mmm," sound and kissed the back of my neck, "Good morning beautiful," he whispered into my ear.

I had been thinking it was a wonderful way to wake up and spend a day and maybe I should run to the kitchen and bring us breakfast in bed. Now, with him awake and aroused, I couldn't help but think that staying in bed making love sounded like a much better plan.

An hour later we were curled up in a sweaty pile both breathing hard and smiling. I kept feeling like I should say something, but I had no idea what to say and the silence felt somehow comforting, like we didn't need to fill the space up with words, that just being here together was enough.

The reverie of our cuddle session was broken by Kail's cell phone ringing.

"Hello."

"Sure, I can do that."

"I need a bit to get ready...say an hour and I'll be at your place?"

"Sounds good, see you then."

He put the phone on the nightstand then squeezed me tightly. "That was one of the guys working on the project with me, he wants me to come over and look at a few things. I need to hop in the shower and get over there," he kissed me softly and then he was gone.

Somehow the whole room felt empty without him in it. Somehow my bed felt cold as soon as he got out of it. Somehow I felt diminished by the lack of him.

That is when the panic set in.

I had just met this guy a couple days before and now we're having sex and literally sleeping together and I am very much in lust if not having the inkling of falling in love and I was leaving soon.

This was not like me at all. I was never this impulsive. I never hopped into bed with a guy this fast. I never had feelings this fast. I also never slept in this late! It was almost noon!

None of this was like me at all and I suddenly didn't know what to do. I had a cold shower, which didn't help. I kept thinking about Kail naked in his shower and how we could have showered together instead.

I threw on my boxers and tank top pajama's and headed downstairs. Kass was in the kitchen having a sandwich while she typed away one handed on her laptop.

"Well look who finally decided to get out of bed! Late night?" her tone was teasing and I could tell she was suppressing a laugh.

I poured myself a cup of coffee and forced myself to keep a straight face as I said in my most serious tone, "Indeed it was. Shall I give you a full report of your bothers lovemaking abilities?"

Within seconds we were both doubled over laughing hysterically. It was at that moment that Kail came downstairs. He glanced at us and said, "I have a sneaking suspicion I am the cause of the laugher. I need to run and don't dare ask. Please don't belittle me in my absence," which only set us both off laughing like hyenas again.

Once we had finally calmed down I asked Kass her feelings about last night's talk with Kail, "Honestly, it was incredible. There is this whole other side to him I never knew about. So many things that if I had known about it could have changed things between us years ago. I think about all the years we missed out on being closer and I want to cry. But, thanks to you, now we have the future to be more like siblings and less like strangers."

Impulsively I leaned over and gave her a big, tight hug. She cleared her throat and said, "Enough sappy sibling stuff. I couldn't help but notice you both seemed to sleep in quite late and came down around the same time. I have a feeling one of you didn't sleep in your own bed last night," her tone was back to being light and full of laughter and I couldn't help but smile and blush in response.

"I'll take that as an admission of guilt," she said as she laughed. "I am so happy you two are hitting it off! At first I was just happy for you, but now I'm happy for him too."

That's when she got a text that lit her whole face up. She handed me her phone and I saw that it was a text from Kail.

> Thank you for butting in and
> pushing Melina and I together.
> She's amazing. I've never felt like
> this about anyone before.
> I think I might be falling. Can you
> tell her I might be late tonight at
> Josh's working on the project but
> that tomorrow I want to spend the
> whole day with her?

Kass squealed in excitement and I felt my face drop.

"Oh no. What's wrong? This should be exciting news, not one that makes you look like your puppy just died."

Without knowing where all the emotion was coming from, I suddenly burst out in tears and words, "This morning I woke up in his arms and it felt great. Then we...did stuff...and that felt amazing. Then he left and I started freaking out. This isn't like me! I don't jump into bed with guys and I don't have feelings like this, especially not just days after meeting a guy. I have to go back home in a while, what happens then? If he thinks he's falling for me and I think I could fall for him then I should stop this now before either of us gets hurt when I go back home. But I don't want to stop! I don't ever want to stop! It feels so right and good that the idea of stopping is physically painful, but the idea of not stopping and then being forced to stop is terrifying. I don't know what to do! This feels so good but it doesn't feel like ME!"

Kass put her arm around my shoulder and hugged me while I cried. Finally she said, "You decided to start following your horoscope instead of your own instincts because you felt that what you were doing wasn't working, right?" I nodded my head yes.

"You came out here to visit on the word of your horoscope and it's something you never would have done on your own, right?" Again I nodded my head yes.

"After spending your whole live kowtowing to your mother's will, you finally stood up to her because your horoscope encouraged you to, right?" Again I nodded yes.

"Well it sounds to me like in the past ten days you've done a lot of things that weren't 'you' things. That's a lot of change in a very short period of time. I kind of think maybe this little panic attack is just all of that change catching up with you. And while I don't personally believe horoscopes are science or fact, I do believe that whatever it takes to discover yourself is worth it. So what did your scope say today?"

I had been so wrapped up in Kail and then by my panic that I had completely forgotten to check out my scope! I pulled away from Kass's comforting embrace, grabbed her laptop and pulled it up in seconds.

~ You need to make a decision. If you don't do it now you won't get the chance again and your dreams may come to nothing ~

I sat staring at the screen for at least a minute before Kass said, "I think you have a choice to make. I hope you remember that change can be good, but it can't all happen at once," and then she left the room so I could think in silence.

I spent most of the day in a withdrawn haze. I baked muffins with Kass, helped her do laundry and tidy up the house, then we headed into the backyard, "Bring your laptop!" she shouted as she headed through the double French doors from the kitchen onto the covered patio.

I brought my laptop down and sat in one of the chairs, balancing it in my lap, and said in a soft voice, "Why did I need to bring this out here?"

Without raising her eyes from her own screen she said, "Because you've been going around here like a zombie for the last couple hours. It's clear you're processing stuff. You do that best when you write. So write!" her tone was firm and brokered no argument. I did as I was told.

I sat and looked at the screen for a couple minutes, and then my fingers began to fly. A minute later I looked over at Kass, "I wrote a poem," I said softly. I felt suddenly raw and exposed.

"Read it to me," she said in that stern voice.

"It's called 'In You I Find'
        In your arms I find
        A sense of peace
        In your kisses I feel
        An undeniable passion
        In your shy smile
        I find a sweet joy
        In your soft touch
        I find acceptance
        In your laughter
        I find friendship"

"It's good, but there's more to write. Keep going."

I wanted to cry from frustration as I looked at the screen. I didn't know what to write. I was a jumble of emotions I had never felt before, how was I supposed to give words to something I had no point of reference for? Finally I took a deep breath, closed my eyes, put my fingers on the keys and started to type.

After a few more minutes I looked over at Kass, "Another one," I said softly. Again she said sternly without looking up from her own screen, "Read it to me."

"It's called 'Your Potential'
 Your arms could be
 My safe haven
 Your eyes could
 Drown me in their depths.
 Your smile could be
 My shelter from the storm.
 Your voice could
 Lull me to the edge.
 You have the potential
 To heal as much as hurt"

"That's better. You're getting closer. Keep going."

I was on the verge of tears now. I let out a growl of frustration, "What do you want from me!?" I demanded.

Then she looked over at me and her face was very serious. "I want you to be honest with yourself about why you're struggling with this. Change is scary, I get that. You've been through a lot of change in the last few days, I get that. But I think after all these years of sharing our most secret thoughts with each other that I have some idea of how you work and I feel like there's something bigger behind your hesitation and panic besides just a lot of change. You can't deal with it until you acknowledge it.

You do that best through your poetry. So write more," she looked back at her screen and it was clear the discussion was over.

I sat for a few minutes thinking about what she had said. Part of me hated to admit it, but she was right. There was something more going on here than just a lot of change being overwhelming. Somewhere inside me was a deep fear that had started to take root and grow since that morning in the pantry. It was time to put that fear into words.

A few minutes later I said softly, "I'm done."

Kass looked over at me and said once more, "Read it."

"It's called 'Afraid To Say'
    Afraid to say anything
    The spoken words
    Will make it too real
    Then I can't take it back
    Afraid you will reject me
    And push me away
    Perhaps even more afraid
    That you will feel the same
    And then there would be
    So much more to lose"

Immediately her face softened and she smiled gently, "Doesn't that feel better?"

I nodded my head yes, but was afraid that if I tried to speak I would start crying.

Kass stood up and reached for my hand, "Let's go inside and have some tea."

I spent the rest of the day and night on pins and needles waiting for Kail to get home. I still wasn't sure what I was going to say or do, but I did know that even though I was terrified, that I needed to keep going. I needed to see where this path would lead us.

It was eleven at night and he wasn't home yet. Kass had gotten a text from him around nine saying he would be a little longer, and I wanted to stay up to talk to him when he got home, but I just couldn't. After a day of feeling like an emotional roller coaster I was exhausted. I said goodnight to Kass and headed to bed.

I was asleep almost as soon as my head hit the pillow.

I knew I was dreaming, but it was so beautiful I didn't want it to be just a dream. There were apple blossoms everywhere; the air was thick with the scent of them. I was in a white gown and veil looking like a princess. Kass was beside me holding a bouquet out to me saying, "It's time," as violins started to play in the distance. Suddenly there was a pathway in front of me. It was long and winding with little twinkling lights leading the way. I started to follow the path and the music got louder the farther I went. I looked up and saw Kail standing at the end of the path. He was wearing a tuxedo and looked so happy.

I walked up to him and he took my hand in his and said, "Melina Alexis Robinson, I love you. I love being with you. I love kissing you. I love holding you. I love listening to you talk and watching you laugh. I want to spend the rest of my life loving you. Will you be my wife?"

Dream me opened her mouth to respond and I waited anxiously to hear her answer. But she seemed frozen like that, about to say something but saying nothing at all.

That's when I heard Kail's disembodied voice, "Melina, are you awake?"

I was suddenly aware of my body and I felt Kail curl up next to me. I was pulled from the fantasy dreamland back into reality. Was the dream a sign that if I followed this path we could get married? Was it showing me I still hadn't made up my mind? I felt so torn and confused and afraid of making the wrong choice.

I turned to face him and he smiled and kissed me softly, "I'm sorry, I didn't mean to wake you up. Go back to sleep," his voice was a soft whisper in the dark and I sighed contentedly as he wrapped his arms around me and kissed my forehead.

In his arms all my fears were banished. All I could think was how good and right this felt. With him next to me all my worries throughout the day felt silly and unfounded. When he kissed my forehead and whispered, "Sweet dreams," I closed my eyes and saw the apple blossoms and knew I had already started to fall for this man and that I would continue to fall for him regardless of my fears.

NOVEMBER 11

As my dream faded and reality set in I found myself in the exact same place. I had dreamed about spending a lazy day at home with Kail, playing video games and board games and cooking together, then making love and falling asleep in each other's arms. As I awoke in his arms I had a sense of having lived a dream and the feeling was wondrous.

I smiled to myself as I snuggled into him, causing parts of him to wake up quickly. This had the desired effect as he nuzzled the back of my neck and let out a soft moan, "Well good morning beautiful," he said before he started kissing the back of my neck.

I relished in the feel, sound and smell of him. I couldn't imagine a better way to wake up, or that the novelty of waking up next to him would ever get old. I turned in his arms and kissed him softly, "Good morning to you too. It's Sunday, any plans?"

He bent his head to nuzzle my neck and chest, his beard tickling me and setting me into a fit of giggles. Once he'd pulled away and I had stopped giggling he kissed my forehead and said, "I do need to finish a homework assignment that's due tomorrow, but other than that my day is free. Any ideas?"

My dream of a lazy day came back to me and it seemed like bliss to be so domestic and casual with him. But it wasn't just the two of us who had to be taken into consideration. There was Kass and Liam too. "How about we hop in the shower then head down for some brunch and see what Kass and Liam have going and figure it out from there?"

"That sounds like a plan...but there's something missing,"

Kail said with a devious twinkle in his eye. "What's that?" I asked somewhat suspiciously.

He lowered his mouth to mine and kissed me once, softly, then moved down to my chin, then my neck and kept kissing lower and lower. "I guess the shower will have to wait," I said breathlessly as I was lost in the sensation of his kisses on my skin.

An hour and a half later the brunch I had mentioned would now officially be lunch. As Kail was in his room putting clothes on I checked my scope.

~ There is a spring in your step and a smile on your face, and with good reason. The best time of the year is about to begin. Enjoy! ~

It seemed the day was destined to be as good as I had dreamed!

I headed to Kail's room and we walked down the stairs hand in hand. We found Kass and Liam sitting at the kitchen table sipping coffee in their pajamas.

"Looks like we aren't the only ones who slept in," I said with a grin on my face as I poured myself a cup of coffee.

"Nope. At least we put on real clothes," Kail said with laughter in his voice as he grabbed his own cup.

"You two can just hush. Sunday's are meant for wearing pajama's all day and sleeping in," Kass said as she nuzzled Liam's neck.

Kass was a very affectionate person, Liam however seemed to be somewhat uncomfortable with public displays of affection. He tolerated Kass's nuzzling but he did not return it. Instead he took a sip of his coffee and almost seemed to blush slightly as he avoided eye contact.

We joined them at the table and I couldn't help but smile. The two of them were so adorable together. I noticed Kass had the same expression on her face and when our eyes met we knew we had both been thinking the same thing and we both burst out laughing.

The guys looked at each other, then the two of us. Complete bewilderment on their faces. "It's okay boys, it was a girl moment," Kass said, still laughing.

I loved how casual and content everything felt. It was as if this whole house and everyone in it was blanketed with happiness. I had never felt so happy and free in my whole life as I did here with these people. I kept pushing the idea of going back to Montana out of my mind. It was "Montana" not "home" because this place felt much more like "home" than anywhere I had ever been.

I was pulled out of my reverie by Kass's voice, "So folks, any plans today?"

"I need to do some work on an assignment but that should only take a couple hours," Kail said as he rubbed his knee against mine under the table.

"I have some work to do to prepare for a meeting tomorrow, but I can do that remotely from here and it should also only take a few hours," Liam said as he smiled at Kass.

"Well we girls have no plans so how about we leave you boys to your work and we head out for lunch and when we get back maybe we can all do something together?"

The guys nodded their heads and Kass stood up, "It's a plan then! I'm sure you two can fend for yourselves to find some lunch while we're gone. Come on Melina, help me pick out something to wear."

In Kass's walk in closet I felt like a bum. Yes, I was wearing a pair of black leggings with a plum tunic style sweater that hugged all my curves and had a deep V neck showing off plenty of cleavage' I knew I looked fashionable and attractive. But Kass had clothes that I would have to save up half a year to afford.

As if she could tell this was what I was thinking she pulled on a pair of faded blue jeans and one of Liam's university sweaters and declared, "I'm ready, let's go!"
I gave her a look that clearly said, 'are you sure?' she just smiled at me and headed towards the garage.

It was a quick ride just a couple blocks to a place called Panera. As soon as we walked in I could smell freshly baked bread and I let out a small sigh. "You okay?" Kass asked, raising her eye brow at me suspiciously.

I blushed a little at my own sentimentality, "I'm fine; I just love the smell of freshly baked bread. It's one of the few nice memories of my childhood. Every Sunday morning my mom would bake two loaves of bread and I loved waking up to the smell and having a fresh slice with breakfast."

"I think that's the first time you've ever said anything genuinely positive about your childhood. It's nice to know there were some good points in there and it wasn't all dreary and maudlin," Kass gave me a quick hug then headed to the counter.

"Can I have the tuna salad please?" the girl behind the

counter smiled and nodded then looked at me. I had only
had a second to glance at the menu so I just ordered the
first sandwich I saw, "Can I get the Roasted Turkey and
Avocado BLT please?"

Once we were seated with our food we dug in. I like
turkey, bacon, lettuce, tomato and avocado so I figured the
sandwich was a pretty safe bet. I did not expect it to be so
delicious! "Oh my! I think this might be the best sandwich
I have ever eaten!" I said as I took another bite and
savored it.

Kass smiled and took a bite of her sandwich, "They do
good work here. So…I could assume things based on the
two of you coming down together this morning, but I
need to hear it from you. What did you decide yesterday?"

I finished my bite and cleared my throat. "I am terrified of
getting hurt or hurting him. I keep trying not to think
about what will happen when I have to go back to
Montana. I am going to just see where this leads. I mean,
we both know I'm leaving in a little while, it's not like it's a
secret or I'm lying or keeping things from him. Yesterday I
was ready to tell him that we had to stop, but then I had
this dream about him and I woke up at a pivotal moment
in the dream and he was in my room and when I'm with
him it all just feels right and good and I'm terrified, but I'm
going to keep following my heart and see where it takes
me."

My awkward monologue done I took a big bite of my
sandwich and stared at my plate, afraid to meet Kass's
gaze.

"Well thank goodness!" she said, relief clear in her voice. I
looked up to find her smiling at me. "I was worried one or
both of you would be too chicken to follow this thing

through. You are both clearly into each other in a big way and you bring out to best in each other. I would be really disappointed if either of you gave up now just because when you leave things will get a little complicated."

I wasn't sure what I was expecting from her, but this was not it. I simply stared at her in astonishment. She smiled back at me sweetly, "I'm no fortune teller, I don't know what will happen. Maybe when you go back to Montana that will be the end. It will have been a fling and you'll both move on. Maybe you two will stay friends. Maybe you will do the long distance relationship thing. I don't know. I don't need to know. All I care about is that you two see where it goes and don't give up because it might get hard. You two are really good for each other and I just want you both to be happy."

Impulsively I leaned over and hugged her. We ate the rest of our lunch while chatting about books and writing. It was casual and carefree, yet somehow I felt that we had shared a significant moment.

After lunch we window shopped at a nearby bookstore to kill some more time before heading back home. It would seem the guys had finished their respective projects because we came home to find them playing Rockband in the living room.

Kass and I watched them play a few songs before we all moved to the upstairs family room for some board games.

After a couple hours of playing Pandemic and saving the world as often as we watched it explode into oblivion being overrun by disease, we headed to the kitchen. The four of us worked together to make a delicious dinner of barbecued ribs, roasted potatoes, salad, corn on the cob and biscuits.

Scope

We ate and chatted and we felt like a family. I had grown
up in a house devoid of affection or laughter. Now I was
surrounded by it. I marveled at how my life had changed in
such a short period of time, and how much happiness I
had found.

After cleaning up from dinner we all played a few more
board games and then all decided to call it a night around
ten.

Kail and I waited for Kass and Liam to go downstairs
before we went into my room. We both knew they both
knew we spent our nights together, but somehow going
into the same bedroom in front of them seemed crass.

We laid in bed talking about the day, then I told him about
my conversation with Kass at lunch. When I was done
telling him what Kass and I had both said he grabbed my
hand, kissed it softly and said, "I don't know where this
will end up either. A long distance relationship doesn't
appeal to me, but not being with you doesn't appeal to me
either. Who knows what will happen when you go back
home. All I know is that while you're here I want to be
with you, and when you leave I will still want to be with
you. That's a bridge we will cross when we get to it. For
now, I just want to enjoy you," then his lips were on mine
and our bodies pressed against one another.

That night we made love. It was intense, emotional,
intimate and amazing. As my body reached highs I had
never imagined, my heart soared and swelled with
emotion. As we pulled apart and lay sweating and
breathing heavily, I felt tears flowing down my face from
the sheer beauty and intimacy of what had just happened.

In that moment I knew that no matter what I had thought
in the past, I had never made love before, and I had never

been in love before. I was no longer falling…I had definitely fallen all the way down the rabbit hole and found myself in a land of happiness and bliss where I handed my heart to him willingly.

NOVEMBER 12

I woke up confused when a strange whirring noise pulled me out of my dream. It sounded like a helicopter, but we were inside.

Then Kail leaned over and kissed my forehead, "I need to get to class. Have a good day and I'll be home around three," he said as he crawled out of bed and made the obnoxious noise stop.

I promptly fell back asleep and dreamed about how wonderful it would be to wake up in his arms every morning.

It was around ten when I woke up on my own. I reached out for Kail and found only a pillow. For a moment my heart sank. Then I remembered the alarm and him leaving for class and I smiled. He had kissed me and wished me a good day. It was the sort of thing you saw on TV. I had never had anyone do that for me. I couldn't imagine my parents doing that for each other. Somehow my life had become a movie where everything was rainbows and sunshine. I had no idea how I had gotten so lucky to find such happiness, but I wasn't going to sit around dissecting it either. I was going to enjoy it as much as possible while it lasted.

I got out of bed and checked my scope as I got dressed.

~ You know instinctively what you should be doing next. Don't waste time, but don't take it too seriously either. Have fun! ~

I wasn't sure what I should be doing next, but perhaps the day would show me. I headed down for breakfast with a smile on my face.

Once again I found Kass sitting at the kitchen table with a coffee in her hand, but she was on the phone.

"I am so sorry Mother Bertrand, I completely forgot. We have an out of town guest staying with us and I got all wrapped up in her visit. I am so sorry. I will make sure Liam is there, we will all be there. And I will make my apple cobbler and a spinach salad, of course. We will be there early to help set up. Thank you," she hung up the phone and put her head in her hands.

"What's wrong?" I asked as I poured my own cup.

"I completely forgot about this family barbecue thing for Liam's side of the family tonight. His mother just called upset that I hadn't RSVP'd. It's in their back yard, it's not like they are booking a hall or anything. I need to call Liam at work and remind him, text Kail at school and tell him he needs to be home by four and then I am going to need your help to get the salad and cobbler and me all ready in time."

I had heard stories about Liam's mother over the years. She was the quintessential Southern Lady who viewed social hierarchy as a serious business and her place in it as the only thing in life that mattered. Liam had been raised wealthy and Kass had been raised middle class. Her mother-in-law never let her forget that she was not one of them and reveled in finding any way to belittle Kass.

I hugged her and said, "Whatever you need, I am on it! Want me to put glass in the cobbler so she dies?"

Kass burst out laughing and hugged me back, "Thanks, I needed that! But, sadly, no. Just brown sugar and oatmeal; no glass this time. We had best get started."

Six hours later and we were loading things into the car. Kass was stunning with her hair in casual waves, her makeup flawlessly applied and wearing a cream colored dress with pale pink flowers on it that hung to her knees and had a modest neckline. The look was finished off with a pearl necklace and matching earrings, a pale pink cardigan and white strappy sandals.

I wore the dressiest and most modest thing I had at my disposal. A knee length green chiffon skirt with a fitted cap sleeved plum blouse. It did have a slight V neck, but it showed the least cleavage of all the shirts I had bought that could possibly go with the skirt. I had no jewelry so Kass lent me a pair of silver teardrop earrings with a matching necklace and I wore my strappy sandals.

Kail sat in the back seat wearing the outfit he had worn on our first official date and was carefully balancing platters of food.

It took us about a half hour to drive to Liam's parents' house. The whole way Kass was a nervous wreck. She kept obsessing about the food and her clothes and hair and kept telling me to smile and nod and not give a personal opinion about anything.

I had thought that Kass and Liam lived in a mansion, but it was nothing compared to the house we pulled up to. It had its own gated street with a footman and its own parking lot! The house was as big as some hotels and was beautiful in gray brick.

As we parked the car a young woman who looked terribly out of place ran up to the car.

She was tall and slender, but curvy. She had flame red shoulder length hair and the brightest blue eyes I had ever seen. She looked out of place because while we had all worn dressy, modest clothing, this girl looked like she was about to go to a punk concert.

She was wearing a dress, but it had a bustier halter top that had her breasts practically spilling out and a flared skirt that stopped mid-thigh. The whole dress was done in red and black plaid. And how she had run across the pavement in the six inch red and black heals I had no idea. I would have killed myself trying to run in those shoes!

"Kass, hurry up! Mother is driving me to the point of matricide! Come save me!!!" She cried as she dramatically flung herself against the driver's side door.

Kass got out of the car and gave the girl a big hug. As I got out of the passenger's side she introduced me, "Melina Alexis Robinson, meet Alexandria Rowena Bertrand. She's Liam's littler sister and one of my best friends. And at this moment I suspect she's given her mother a heart attack with that outfit," Kass laughed as she took in the full effect of the outfit, "All that's missing is bright red lipstick and thick black eyeliner."

"I had it on but mother came at my face with a baby wipe and took it all off. I plan to reapply once people start showing up and she's distracted."

"You are so wicked! I can't wait to see Mother Bertrand's reaction!" Kass said as she started handing Alexandria dishes from the back seat. The two of them headed towards the giant house as Kail and I followed.

The house was massive. Every space seemed designed to make you feel small. The kitchen was bigger than my whole apartment back home. I held Kail's hand like a lifeline as we followed Kass.

The two were chattering nonstop, talking so fast I could hardly follow. It was even harder as neither of them seemed to finish a sentence; the other would just say "I know!" and they would move on. They busied themselves in the kitchen while Kail and I held hands and huddled together in the corner trying to stay out of the way.

Then *she* walked in. Without having ever seen a picture of her or even had her physically described to me, I knew it was Liam's mother. She was tall and thin with strawberry blond hair lightly streaked with white gray. She had a regal bearing about her, emphasized by wearing a skirt suit that looked like something the Queen would wear as well as having the same hair style. She started giving orders in a firm but soft voice. This was a woman who never needed to raise her voice because even her softest whisper was immediately obeyed.

"Kassia, Alexandria, can the two of you please get out of the kitchen and let the servants do their jobs. I am not paying them to watch the two of you work," I had known Kass's full name was Kassia, but had never heard anyone use it before. Then she turned to us, "You two, who are you and why are you in my kitchen?"

The two of us stared, like deer's in the headlights. Thankfully Kass came to our rescue, "Mother Bertrand, you remember my brother, Kail. And this is my friend Melina who is visiting from Montana."

"Well you two do not need to be in my kitchen either. Anyone who is not staff, out of the kitchen now," she said and turned away from us on her heal.

Alexandria walked up and took us both by the hand and said loudly, "Come on K, Mel, I'll give you the grand tour!" and led us from the room.

I stuttered out, "Um…Alexandria…I don't go by Mel…just…just Melina," as I had to keep you with Alexandria's brisk pace.

She turned to me and smiled, "Mother hates nicknames, so around here you go by Mel. And I never go by Alexandria, so please call me Lex. And welcome to the humble Bertrand abode. Come into my parlor, said the spider to the fly," and she turned and walked down the hall, leaving us to scramble to follow after her.

Lex led us into a large formal sitting room where she plopped down unceremoniously onto a sofa, "Man I can't wait for this night to be over!" she sighed.

"I wish your mother did less of these things; or at least stopped inviting us. The only one she really wants here is Liam," Kass said as she collapsed next to Lex.

Lex seemed so out of place here. So different from her mother or Liam. I wondered if this was some sort of rebellion, of if this was genuinely who she was.

Suddenly a disembodied voice came out of nowhere, "Mrs. Kassia Bertrand, your husband has arrived and is requesting your presence and that of your brother in the library post haste." It was a man's voice, deep and monotone with a hint of a British accent and dripping with condescension.

Kass saw the look of confusion on my face as I glanced around the room, "It's an intercom system throughout the house. Mother Bertrand likes to have full authority everywhere at all times. That was the voice of her head butler, Simon. I guess I'll leave you in Lex's capable hands while we go see what Liam wants," Kass got up and led Kail out the door. He turned as he walked out and gave me an expression that clearly said, 'don't leave me alone with these people!' and I had to smile as I blew him a kiss.

Once they were out the door Lex came over and plopped down next to me. "Before you have too much time to wonder or assume, here's the scoop," she said as she deftly started to apply eyeliner without a mirror.

"I have always been the black sheep since I was born. I inherited the red hair my mother always hated in herself. I did everything early - walking, talking, that sort of thing - so I was a source of pride. Until I could put together full sentences at age three and I started saying things my mother didn't like. When I was four she was having tea with all the social queens of the state and I walked in, completely naked, and said 'Mama, I will not wear any of my clothes. They all look like yours and yours are ugly!' and I walked out. She was mortified and never forgave me for embarrassing her in front of her high society friends. Liam was ten when I was born and he had always done as he was told and worshiped her. Once she realized I would not be a little clone of her, she basically forgot about me. She let the servants raise me and as I got older she threw money at me to keep me out of sight and out of mind. But in society you can't hide because everyone is watching and everyone remembers. So to get me to come out to these damned events she pays me one hundred dollars an hour to smile and nod and not cause too much of a stir."

She must have seen the disapproval on my face that she would accept money for something like that from her own mother. She smiled and said, "Don't worry, I donate all the money I get for these things to a local charity for runaway teens, but Mother doesn't need to know that, she winked at me conspiratorially and I had to laugh.

"I came out publicly as being a lesbian a couple years ago, so now it's popular for me to be at events to give Mother more of a politically correct edge. Which is fine with me since now I can donate more money to charity. If I bring a date I charge her two hundred an hour," she started chuckling as she applied her lipstick.

Once she was all done up she turned to me and smiled, "So with all that out of the way…any questions to clear the air?"

I was still trying to process the fact that this young woman was a lesbian. I had never known anyone who wasn't heterosexual. All I knew came through sitcoms and movies. I had always imagined lesbians to be the stereotypical "butch" women who were overly masculine with short hair, no makeup, jeans and baggy shirts. This young woman was very feminine and didn't meet any of the stereotypes I had come to associate with lesbians.

She smiled at me and said softly, "Am I your first lesbian?"

I blushed and looked away, embarrassed at seeming like a backwards country bumpkin. I had lived a sheltered life and now it was showing. She patted my arm lightly and said in a kind tone, "It's okay dear. Everyone has a first encounter eventually. I'm guessing right now you're trying to fit me into the box in your head marked 'Lesbian' and I'm not fitting and you don't know what to do with me?"

I still couldn't look her in the eye; instead I hung my head and stared into my lap. Full of embarrassment I nodded my head yes.

Then I felt her hand on my chin, forcing me to life my head and turn to face her. She looked me straight in the eyes and said in a voice which was firm, but kind, "I am attracted to women, I sleep with women, but other than that I am just like everyone else. I have the same goals, hopes and dreams as any other woman. Just replace the husband with a wife. I am open about my sexuality because I feel I should not have to hide who I am, not because I want deferential treatment. I am the same as everyone else and I expect to be treated as everyone else is. Whatever you would do or say to Kass I hope you would feel comfortable doing and saying with me. I am just a person," then she patted my cheek and said, "Is my makeup okay? I don't look like The Joker do I?"

I couldn't help but smile and laugh. Somehow in the midst of an incredibly embarrassing and awkward situation she managed to keep the mood light and carefree. Her smile was contagious and her laugh infectious. "Your makeup is perfect. I don't know how you do it without a mirror in minutes like that! I can't do it that well with a mirror and an hour to try!"

She smiled sweetly, "Years of practice my dear," then her expression turned more serious, "So, before this night gets underway and we are forced to mingle and rub elbows with snobby people who we aren't allowed to actually talk to…any questions?"

I blushed again. My mind was whirling with a ton of questions, all very personal and inappropriate and I didn't have the courage to ask any of them.

Then I remembered my scope…I instinctively knew what I should be doing next. Right now my gut was saying this was neither the time nor the place to talk about these things with Lex, but that I really wanted to talk to her about them. It also said not to waste time, but not to take it too seriously. So right now might not be the best option, but that didn't mean never.

I took a deep breath and said it before I could stop myself, "Honestly, I have a ton of questions. All of them feel very personal and inappropriate and right now seems like the worst possible time to start asking them. But maybe one day this week we could get together, hang out and talk?"

Lex smiled, "Of course we can dear. Don't worry about being inappropriate. Being a lesbian is sort of like being pregnant. When you're pregnant complete strangers think it's okay to walk up and touch your body without permission. When you're an out lesbian people you hardly know or have just met think it's okay to ask incredibly personal questions. I got used to it years ago. I'm also a really open person. So don't worry your pretty little head about being inappropriate, just be honest and I'll do the same. Okay?"

I nodded my head yes and blushed, still embarrassed by my lack of exposure to these things. Lex smiled and said, "You are so adorable when you blush. Makes you seem all sweet and innocent. I see why Kail is so keen on you," then she winked at me and stood up. She smoothed her dress down and gave a resigned sigh, "For now, we had best join the party before Mother has a conniption and sends Simon to find us."

Kass, Lex and Kail may have thought of the night as a dreadful inconvenience and a bore. To me it was like living in a movie. Everything and everyone was so fancy and posh. And while Kass and Lex may have felt restricted by having to smile, nod and bite their tongues, I was relieved. I had no idea what I would have said to any of those people if I had been expected to voice an opinion.

Liam mingled and hobnobbed with Kass on his arm, making business connections and being the perfect socialite son. Lex spent the night flitting from group to group, smiling and strutting proudly, clearly enjoying making people uncomfortable with her overflowing breasts. In her six inch heals she was around six feet tall, causing her bountiful breasts to be at eye level of many of the guests. When she felt she had made one group sufficiently uncomfortable she would bounce over to the next.

Kail and I clung to each other the whole night, never letting go of each other's hands. We smiled and nodded and when our only responses were mumbled hellos, agreements and goodbye's people stopped trying to socialize with us.

I was in awe of everything around me and was trying to soak it all in. I wished I could pull out my camera phone and start taking pictures like a tourist, but somehow I suspected that Mother Bertrand would not approve.

While I was looking all around m trying not to gawk, I found that all night my eyes kept being pulled back to Lex. I could find her in the crowd in a single breath and when I felt she was distracted enough not to notice, I would simply stare at her in wonder as I squeezed Kail's hand like a lifeline.

The entire car ride back to the house Kass talked about how Mother Bertrand had questioned her wardrobe and complained about Lex. I was too lost in trying to remember every detail of the night to pay much attention.

We all worked together to get all the dishes into the kitchen. Once the last item had been brought in Kass gave a big sigh and said, "I could go for a soak in the hot tub. Anyone want to join me?"

Kail came up behind me and put his hands on my hips as he rested his head on my shoulder and said, "I could go for that."

I hadn't been aware of feeling keyed up or aroused throughout the day or evening, but as soon as he pressed against me and touched me, my body was on fire. I literally swooned with the power of my desire as I felt every nerve in my body throb. I put my hands over his and gave a light squeeze as I said, "Not me, thanks. I'm going to turn in early," and I turned and bolted up the stairs.

I was standing next to my bed, frantically taking my clothes off when Kail came in the room with a bewildered look on his face. He saw me standing naked by the bed and a slow grin creped across his face, "Did you get a little worked up at the party?" he said with a hint of mockery in his voice as he walked towards me.

Once he was within arm's reach I grabbed hold of his belt and started working it off, "I wasn't worked up at all until you touched me. So really, this is all your fault. So it's your responsibility to fix it," my voice was already hoarse with lust as I frantically worked to remove his pants.

"I think I could probably help you out with that," he said with laughter in his voice as he stepped out of his pants.

I didn't really know how my hormones had gone from zero to sixty, but by this point he had was taking off his shirt and the how no longer mattered. All that mattered was his body against mine, his lips on my skin, and the sound of our hearts beating frantically together.

NOVEMBER 13

I woke up and stretched, long and languid. I wondered if this was what it felt like to be a cat; to feel boneless and fluid in your own body. I grinned at the thought and from the bathroom door Kail chuckled and said, "You look like the cat that ate the canary. Enjoyed last night did you?"

I smiled at him and sighed, "Mmm hmm," as I continued to stretch, giving him a view of my body naked on the bed as I wriggled around.

My little show had the desired effect and in moments he was next to me on the bed, holding me in his arms as he kissed me passionately.

I felt like an addict. I couldn't get enough of his touch or his kisses. It was as if without them I was drowning and only his touch or kiss could bring me above the water and let me breathe again.

Suddenly I no longer felt aroused. Instead I felt overwhelmed and afraid, like a child in the dark. I pulled away from Kail's kisses and when he saw the look on my face he backed off, "What is it? What's wrong? What did I do?" his voice was soft and tinged with fear and concern.

I gently stroked his cheek as I felt a tear roll down my own, "You didn't do anything. It's just me. I…I don't know…I'm just feeling so much and thinking so much and it's all new to me and I don't understand any of it."

He pulled my hand from his cheek and gently kissed it, "It's okay and it makes perfect sense. I'm going through the same thing. I've never felt this way before. I've never thought these things. I have no idea what I'm doing and I'm afraid of screwing up."

We laid there for a while. Silent. Just holding each other and taking comfort in the closeness and touch of another person who was as confused and lost as we felt.

Our reverie was broken when Kass knocked on the door, "Kail, we have that lunch thing with mom. I want to leave in an hour; you'd best finish what you're doing and get ready."

We listened to her walk down the hall and stairs before we turned to each other. "I guess I've got to get dressed and head out," he said as he brushed a piece of my hair away from my face.

Fearing that if I tried to speak I would start to cry, I simply nodded my head in agreement.

"Are you okay?" again I simply nodded yes.

"Are we okay?" at that I leaned forward and kissed him softly before nodding my head yes.

The look on his face made it clear that he didn't believe me, but that he felt he had no choice but to take me at my word. He looked into my eyes for a moment before he said softly, "Okay. I'm going to shower and get ready, but when I get back tonight I'd like to talk about this a little more, if you're up for it?"

I whispered, "Okay," as I fought the growing wave of emotion building inside me.

I watched him get out of bed, pull on his boxers and leave my room before I let the first tear fall. I was afraid if he knew how fast and far I was falling for him that he would run away. I was afraid of how much I craved him, not just sexually, but to simply be near him, to see him and spend time with him. I was afraid of how much my body was drawn to him.

After I had soaked the pillow with a river of silent tears, I washed my face with cold water, threw on my nightshirt and checked my scope before going in search of coffee.

~ Be your truest self today and let people see all the good in you. There is no reason to hide who you are. Stop holding back ~

How was I supposed to be my truest self when I didn't even know who my truest self was? How could I stop holding back when I was so afraid of everything I felt? How could there be no reason to hide who I am when I felt a rising fear inside myself that letting my thoughts and feelings out into the open would somehow ruin everything and condemn me back to the outskirts of life once more?

I closed my eyes and took a long, slow, deep breath to clear my mind. Today's scope was one that was hard to swallow, but I would do my best. I had promised myself to make changes, I had come so far and I couldn't run away now. I needed coffee.

Still in my nightshirt I headed to the kitchen. Kass was sitting at the table doodling on a notepad and said in her bright, chipper voice, "Good morning!" I mumbled "Morning" back to her as I made a B-line for the coffee pot.

I sat down in the chair next to her and started sipping. I could feel her eyes on me, but didn't dare meet them.

"Is everything okay? Both of you have come down here looking like zombies this morning. Did you have a fight?"

I shook my head no and said, "We're good. Just both a little overwhelmed. I don't know. None of it makes sense."

I heard a car horn from the garage and Kass jumped up, "I've got to run before he leaves in my car. We'll talk tonight, okay?"

I mumbled agreement as I continued to avoid her gaze. As she was almost out of the kitchen she turned and said, "I almost forgot! I asked Lex to come keep you company while we're out. She should be here soon. Try to have a good day darling!"

I was just stepping out of the shower when I heard Lex calling out, "Hey Mel, you around?"

I quickly threw a towel around myself and ran to open my door and call down the stairs, but when I threw open the door and shouted, "I'll be right down!" Lex was standing about two feet from my door facing me.

Her strawberry blond hair was crimped within an inch of its life and looked wild. She had heavy black eyeliner with a soft green shadow, glossy lips and flawless skin. She was wearing a pair of blue lace leggings and an oversized bright purple tank top that said in bold pink letters "FREE HUGS" she looked young, vibrant, hip and carefree and I was completely taken aback by being so close to her so unexpectedly.

I blushed bright red, "Sorry!" I said in a small, meek voice.

I was embarrassed for practically yelling in her face and for standing in front of her in nothing but a towel. I couldn't stop blushing and couldn't seem to think of anything to say. I was just standing there, frozen.

We stood there staring at each other for almost a minute before Lex broke the silence with a smile, "Why don't you go put some clothes on and then we'll have something to eat?"

I nodded dumbly and closed my door. I took off the towel and collapsed on the bed. My heart was beating a mile a minute and I still felt flushed. I laid there trying to get myself under control for a couple minutes. What was wrong with me? Why did I feel like a shy little kid who had been called into the principal's office whenever she was around?

The idea of spending even an hour alone with her made me incredibly anxious. She was so unpredictable and that made me nervous. My instinct around her was to be like a rabbit in the wild…sit very still and hope she didn't notice me and would pass me by without incident.

But Kass adored her and I trusted Kass's judgment of people. And Liam was her brother so she couldn't be completely crazy. If they had left us alone together they must believe that on some level we would get along.

I took a deep breath to calm myself and got dressed. I threw on a pair of jeans and a fitted, v-neck t-shirt that had a barren tree outline and a bunch of inspirational words all over it. I threw my wet hair up into a lose bun and headed downstairs.

Lex had pulled out bagels, chesses, meats, condiments and all the produce she could find, "I figured we'd do bagel sandwiches with fruit and veggies. Is that okay?" I gave a small smile and nodded as I sat down.

We assembled our sandwiches and ate in silence. I didn't even risk a glance at her for fear she would catch me staring like an idiot. I had no idea what to say to her and I was terrified of what might come out of my mouth if I tried.

After we'd each had our fill, we silently cleaned up the kitchen together. Then we stood across from each other, both leaning against the counters, not saying a word.

Lex cleared her throat loudly then said, "Is it just me, or is it a bit awkward in here?" I couldn't help it; I smiled and glanced up at her.

When our eyes met she smiled brightly, "There we go! Now that you're able to look at me like a real person, what say we go sit down and have a little chat?"

Before I could answer she had grabbed my hand and was pulling me towards the living room.

She sat me down in one of the chairs and sat herself on the sofa. "So, Mel, when we met I asked if you had any questions. You said you did but it wasn't the time or place. Well now we have a couple hours together, so I think it's a pretty good time and place. Ask me anything."

I sat there dumbly like a lump. My brain had suddenly gone blank and I couldn't think of a single thing to say. After about a minute of silence and my blank expression Lex leaned forward, patted my arm lightly and said, "I know I can seem a little…over the top, 'larger than life' if you will. Some people say it's intimidating and makes them feel they can't talk to me. Believe me; no one should be intimidated by me. I'm intimidated by most people, you included."

Me? Why on earth would this confident, beautiful, vibrant, charming young woman be at all intimidated by me?

Stop holding back my scope had said. Fine!

"Why would you be intimidated by me?" I asked in a small voice.

Lex smiled sweetly at me, "Are you kidding? You are taking this huge leap of faith on this adventure; I don't think I'd ever have the balls to do something like this! Not to mention how much Kass has talked up your talent for writing, and I'm a talentless hack. Then there's the fact that you need to look in a mirror more often. What I wouldn't give to have eyes like yours instead of my squinty little eyes! And such thick, luscious hair! Mine is so thin and boring. And not to squeak you out or anything…but you have a great ass! I can only imagine how many girls would be banging down my door if I had a booty like that!"

I was sure I was making the goldfish face again. How could she possibly sit there and think those things of me when she was so stunning?

I could feel the blush creep up my cheeks and I saw Lex's mouth twitch to hide a smile as she noticed; "Now you know there's no reason to be shy. So come on, out with it. Ask me anything."

I sat for a moment and then the words started to rush out, "How do you go around looking like that and not feel like everyone is staring at you? Where do you get all this confidence from? Is this really you, or is this a persona you've created to mess with your mother? How did you find out you're a lesbian? Have you tried being with guys? What's it like being a lesbian? What's it like being out? What was it like coming out? Do you really have gaydar?"

When I had exhausted all the questions that had been flying through my mind I took a deep breath and suddenly felt embarrassed. Lex was smiling gently at me and looked so sweet and kind and I was sure all of my questions had been far too personal and offensive, "Oh my goodness I am so sorry! I shouldn't have said any of that! Forget I said anything!"

I hung my head in my hands from embarrassment as I felt my face turn bright red. I felt like such a fool!

"It's okay, you didn't ask me anything I haven't been asked before," Lex said in a soothing voice. I looked up to find her sitting cross legged on the floor beside my chair. She took both my hands in hers, looked up at me and said, "I told you the other night that I would answer any question you asked. I meant it. It's also true that I've been asked all of those things many times. It's okay Mel, don't worry. I'm not upset or offended or hurt by your questions. Let's go through them one by one shall we?"

She nodded her head encouragingly as she smiled at me sweetly, "Okay," I said in a soft whisper.

"Good! Now, first things first…I think it was how do I look like this and not feel like everyone is watching me? The answer is…I don't. It's true that a large majority of people are so wrapped up in their own lives they don't notice much that goes on around them. Those people might glance at me, but not stop thinking about themselves long enough to even register that there's much different about me. The rest of the people will notice. Some stare, some gawk. Depending on my outfit, sometimes people even approach me and ask to take their picture with me. I don't see the point in being who you are in private and trying to be someone else in public. I am who I am twenty four seven and if other people like it, great! If they don't, that's okay. I'm doing it for me, not them. But I do leave the house every morning knowing that some people will pass me by without even noticing, and others will notice, and I'm okay with that. Any follow up questions to that one?"

I shook my head no, but still couldn't meet her eyes.

"Okay, good. Next was where my confidence comes from. I don't really know what to say to that one. My brother grew up being told he was perfection incarnate, so his confidence comes from being told he's great and then when he is great it's validation and only grows his confidence. From a young age it was clear I was not at all perfect and I was frequently told how imperfect I was. I suspect my confidence comes from a lack of caring. When you're told how imperfect you are all the time you get to a point where you have to stop caring what those people think or you will drive yourself mad. I stopped caring what my mother and her socialite friends thought of me when I was about ten. Since then I've had a lot more confidence. How's that?"

"That actually makes perfect sense," I said excitedly as a light went off in my mind. "When I left for this trip and told my parents I sort of did the same thing. I was finally able to stand up to my mother and be confident and strong because I knew it was what I wanted and I didn't care if she disapproved."

Lex smiled, "Liberating ain't it?" she chuckled and I couldn't help but smile back.

"I think you asked if this is really me or just me messing with mother? Honestly, it's a little of both. Some things developed because I did them to mess with her and then discovered how much I liked them. Like my love of nude sun tanning. I started doing it on the lawn at sixteen to piss her off. But once I did it I realized I loved the feeling of the sun all over my body and not having tan lines. It's actually one of my favorite things to do to relax. I still do it as much as possible even though she doesn't know about it now. And sometimes, if I know I'll be seeing her or one of her society ladies, I'll put a little extra umph into my look. Nothing I wouldn't do on my own, but just a little more eye liner or a slightly shorter skirt or something. But really it's just me."

I nodded my head in understanding and glued my eyes to the floor. The next questions were far more personal and I was nervous and afraid.

"Now we get to the stuff about my being a lesbian. Here's some rapid fire answers for you and then I'll do the more in depth ones," Lex took a deep breath and launched right in.

"Have I tried being with guys? Yes…three of them to be exact.
What's it like being a lesbian? It is what it is. What's it like being straight? You just are what you are.
What's it like being out? It's hard and scary and liberating all at the same time.
Do I have gaydar? No, I'm horrible and always seem to fall for straight girls."

Having spent all her breath in one go, Lex took a couple deep breaths to recover. I continued to stare at the ground until she spoke again.

"How did I find out I was a lesbian? I was seventeen and I had dated a couple boys at school and lost my virginity the year before. I liked both the guys, we were friends and I liked hanging out with them and spending time with them. I even liked some of the physical stuff like hugging and cuddling with them. But the sexual stuff…the kissing,

touching, and sex…it didn't excite me. I didn't get turned
on, I never climaxed, and I was thinking there was
something wrong with me. Then I met David. He was
nineteen and in college. He was sweet and sensitive and
kind and we had so much in common. We became really
good friends and then he asked me to be his girlfriend. I
loved him as a friend, and back then I thought that was
what romantic love felt like, so I said yes.
We had been dating for about two months when he
brought me home to meet his family over the Christmas
holidays. He had a twin sister who had gone away for
college. She was home visiting and was a lot like him. She
was sweet and sensitive and we also had a lot in common.
And she was a lesbian. We never talked about her
sexuality; we just hung out as friends. She never made a
pass at me; I never caught her checking me out or anything
like that. But without my knowing it, David had talked to
her about us. He had told her that we loved each other,
but there was nothing between us in the bedroom. That no
matter what he did I didn't seem to enjoy anything or ever
get aroused, that sex was always painful for me because of
it and that he felt like he was in love with me but I wasn't
in love with him.
One day when we were driving to the store to pick up
some groceries she broached the subject. She jokingly
asked me if her brother was as much of a stud in the sack
as he always bragged about being. I burst into tears.
We parked the car and I told her about my two other
boyfriends and how I had never been turned on and never
had an orgasm and thought I was broken. She asked if I
had ever had an orgasm by myself and I said yes. She
asked what I had been thinking about when it happened
and I told her that I had found my brother's stash of porn
when he was out of town and had watched some. Most of
it did nothing for me, but there was a scene with a man
and two women and it got me turned on and I got myself
off," Lex paused and I looked up at her. Her eyes were

focused on the coffee table, but the look in them was miles away.

Her voice got soft and tender as she continued, "I remember she smiled at me then, the way a mother smiles at a child who can't grasp the concept of the earth being round as they look at a globe. She asked me if I could remember a time with any of the men I had been with when looking at them ever turned me on. I confessed that I hadn't. Then she took off her shirt and bra and I was staring at her sitting there topless. I couldn't take my eyes off her breasts. I had this irresistible urge to touch her skin, it looked so soft. I closed my eyes to try and focus and I pictured myself kissing along her collar bone. I opened my eyes again and she was just sitting there, topless, looking at me and waiting to see what I would say or do. We sat there for a while in silence. Then she asked if looking at anyone had ever turned me on. I said yes. She asked when. I said now. She smiled and grabbed her shirt to put it back on. I reached out and stopped her. That's how I found out I was a lesbian."

Listening to her tell the story was mesmerizing. I felt as if I were in a trance and could feel what she felt. When she stopped talking I was jolted back to reality. Lex was sitting with her eyes focused on the past and a small smile on her lips. I stayed silent while she relived the memories and let her come back to reality in her own time.

Eventually she blinked and her eyes focused on the here and now. She shook her head slightly as if clearing away the shadow of the past, and then she smiled shyly at me and blushed, "Sorry, I got a little lost in the memory there."

I smiled back, "It's okay, I didn't experience it and I got lost in it too. It sounds like she was a pretty phenomenal girl. Though a little awkward with you dating her brother and all."

Lex laughed and her eyes lit up, "She was amazing. My first girlfriend. I've never met anyone else like her. And David was pretty amazing too. You'd think it would have been awkward, but I think he had suspected and that's why he talked to her about it. He was actually very supportive of us being together."

"Do you know that when you talk about her, you get this certain tone in your voice and look in your eyes?" I said softly. I was worried about getting too personal or bringing up painful memories, but I couldn't help myself.

Lex smiled again, but this time there was sadness in it, "I know I do. I always have. She was really the first person I ever loved in any romantic way. We ended on good terms and have stayed friends, as have David and I, but I never stopped loving her."

We sat in silence for a little while. Lex was remembering the past and her first love; while I was thinking about the present and the fact that I had a growing feeling I was afraid to admit out loud.

Kail was my first real love.

After a few minutes Lex clapped her hands to snap us both out of our melancholy thoughts, "That's all well and good and melodramatic, but you had one more question in there. You asked about my coming out. In a nutshell…it was anticlimactic. I had expected theatrics from my mother, indifference from Liam and shock from my friends. Instead mother's response was a cold, 'I shouldn't have expected anything normal or acceptable from you, I shouldn't be surprised by this'. Liam was taken aback and needed a bit of time to adjust, but once he did he ended up being surprisingly supportive. And even though my being a lesbian came as a total shock to me, somehow none of my friends seemed very surprised by it or at all phased by it. So, did I sufficiently answer all of your questions?"

Lex seemed calm and still completely comfortable with my incredibly personal questions. I was baffled by how easily she could open up to someone so much. Yes, I had been vetted by Kass, but I was still essentially a stranger and she had shared so much with me.

"Yes, you did. And thank you. I am in awe of how well you have handled my incredible social blunders and intrusion into your personal life and appreciate it so much," I said softly, emotion in my voice showing how moved I was.

Lex stood up and moved over to where I was sitting. She bent down and gave me a big hug, "Not at all dear. Friends?" I gave her a squeeze back, "Friends!"

Kass and Kail's lunch with their mom turned into a six hour event. When they finally got home they found us laughing and joking as we made a horrible ruckus attempting to play Rockband.

Kass laughed and snuck past us into her room to change. Kail sat down on the couch and watched us play with a big smile on his face.

When we finished the song I walked over and straddled him on the couch, "What is so funny mister?" I said, trying to sound stern, but the grin on my face betrayed me.

He laughed and wrapped his arms around me, pulling me

into him so we were completely pressed against each other; thighs, hips, groins, stomachs, chests and noses. He gave me an eskimo kiss, then laughed and said, "Nothing, your just adorable and I can't seem to be around you without smiling," then he softly kissed the tip of my nose.

The moment was so sweet, tender and intimate that I felt overwhelmed by emotions. My heart was bursting in my chest. My knees went weak.

I blinked slowly and took a deep, cleansing breath. I felt as if I was drowning in emotions too deep for me to comprehend. Part of me wanted to dive right in. Part of me was terrified of being swallowed up.

I pulled away from Kail and turned to run away.

Suddenly Lex grabbed my arm and spun me around, "Where are you going? What's wrong?" she asked, concern and confusion all over her face.

I had completely forgotten she was there, that Kass was home, that anyone but Kail and I existed. I blushed crimson and leaned in close to whisper to her, "I need to get out of here."

Lex looked concerned, but she nodded her head and whispered back, "Go to the backyard, I'll be down in a minute."

As I left the room I heard her saying something about needing to talk to me in private.

I was curled up in a ball on one of the patio sofa's when Lex came outside. She sat down beside me and said in a calm voice, "Wanna tell me what's wrong?"

I took a deep breath and then started to cry.

She hugged me tightly and let me cry until there were no more tears left. Then she patted my back and said softly, "Now that all the tears are out of the way, wanna try words?"

I took a few minutes to try and form coherent thoughts from all the emotions I had been feeling. Finally I started to speak in a voice hoarse from crying, "What you were saying earlier, about your ex being your first love, I can relate. I've had two boyfriends and I guess I felt something for each of them, but nothing even close to what I feel with Kail."

"Ahhhh," she said as she smiled warmly at me, "You're falling for him and it's freaking you out?"

I nodded my head yes.

"Because it's something you've never felt before?"

"Partly. It's all new and so much more overwhelming than I ever thought it would be. I feel like I have no control over my own thoughts or feelings anymore because he controls them all, even when he's not around."

She nodded her head in understanding, "What's the other part?"

"I admit, I had idly wondered what it'd be like to have a fling while I was down here. I've never had a fling before. So when things started happening with him that's what I thought it would be, just a fling. But what I feel is not a fling. I'm so afraid of how much it's going to hurt when I go home. This thing grows every day and then one day I'm just going to leave and it'll be over and that scares me so much. And what if for him it's just a fling and he doesn't care that I leave but I go home all broken, how will I recover?"

Lex hugged me tightly, "Oh hunny if you think this is just a fling for him, you're blind and stupid."

I laughed, and the laughing helped ease some of the pressure in my chest.

"It's not like Kail and I are friends, we've hardly ever spoken to each other; but anyone can see in how he looks at you, how he touches you, that he is crazy about you. And I get how scary it can be to fall for someone, especially when there's a deadline on your time together, but I believe that the pursuit of love is worth the risks. You don't know how things will turn out, but you know how you feel now. Believe in that feeling and see where it leads you."

We sat in silence as I mulled over what Lex had said. She made some valid points, but I was still terrified.

I closed my eyes, took a deep breath, and pictured myself in Kail's arms. Just imagining it made me feel warm and gooey inside. I was terrified of all the what if's and unknown's, but I couldn't turn off this feeling for him.

I took a deep breath and hugged Lex, "Thanks. I'm still terrified, but I can't let that stop me."

She shouted, "Atta girl!" as I headed back inside.

I walked into Kail's room and found him lying in bed reading a text book. I took off my clothes, crawled into bed next to him, and within minutes I was fast asleep.

NOVEMBER 14

When I woke up in his arms the room was pitch black. It had been just after seven when I had crawled into the bed and fallen asleep. I was guessing it was around one in the morning, and I was suddenly wide awake with Kail snoring softly beside me.

I tried to fall back asleep, but after about a half hour of lying there staring at the ceiling I had to accept that it was just not going to happen.

I got out of bed as quickly and quietly as possible. I threw on my boxer shorts and tank top, grabbed my laptop and headed for the kitchen.

I made myself some tea, grabbed a scone and set up my laptop at the table. After about an hour of surfing the internet for anything to entertain me, I realized it would be after midnight back home. Perhaps the paper had updated the scopes for the new day already.

Sure enough they had! Being my true self and not holding back yesterday had been a whirlwind. I was hoping today would be a calmer day.

~ Reflect, think, and consider alternatives you would normally dismiss. Falling down the rabbit hole doesn't have to be a bad thing ~

What was I supposed to reflect about? What alternatives was I dismissing? When did I suddenly become Alice?

I rested my chin in my hands as I stared at the screen, willing the words to somehow magically make sense.

"The Matrix has you. Take the red pill!"

I squealed and jumped in my chair before turning to see where the voice had come from.

It turned out that Lex had come into the kitchen from the backyard through the doors behind me, "You scared the crap out of me!" I tried to yell while still whispering.

She was trying too hard to stifle her laughter to say anything, which only infuriated me more, "Why are you still here? Why didn't you go home?" I demanded, feeling I was somehow defending the honor of the household.

Lex sat down at the table beside me and finally got her laughter under control, "After you and Kail left to molest each other, Kass and I watched a movie and had some wine. She said I could stay the night rather than drive home after having a few glasses. I couldn't sleep so I went outside to dip my feet in the hot tub. What are you doing up? Shouldn't you still be upstairs with your man?"

"I went upstairs and crashed right away. He's still sleeping, but I woke up a while ago and just couldn't get back to sleep. I had hoped some tea would help, but I'm still wide awake."

"You should try the hot tub; it always puts me to sleep."

"I don't think dipping my feet in the hot tub will make me tired, but thanks," even I had to admit my tone on that one was pretty snarky. Thankfully, Lex didn't seem to notice.

"Usually it's a good twenty minute soak to put me to sleep, but I don't have a suit with me and I never go in naked if people are home," when the shock showed on my face she winked at me and I had to laugh.

"I don't know if you're serious or joking, but a soak does sound like a good idea. I don't have a swimsuit though."

Lex glanced down at herself, still in her Free Hugs tank top and lace leggings, and then she looked at me in my boxers and tank top, "We could always go in as we are. It's not like either of us is wearing a whole lot."

The idea was very appealing. Thinking about soaking in the hot tub sounded very relaxing and like something that could very well help me fall asleep again. And the idea of being out in the brisk November air while in the embrace of the hot water gave me goosebumps. But then my logical mind kicked in, "What would we wear afterward though?"

Suddenly Lex's face lit up, "The guest robes!" she said as she stood up and ran out of the kitchen.

I was completely confused until she came back a minute later carrying two white robes. "They keep a few in the laundry room with the spare towels for when guests come to stay. Come on, let's go!"

We raced to the hot tub, laughing as we went. I couldn't help but think that it was a good thing that Kass and Liam had such a big lot so hopefully we wouldn't wake any neighbors.

The water felt amazingly comforting and relaxing. I gave into the warm embrace and let the jets work my tense muscles.

I was vaguely aware of Lex next to me and I could hear her voice as she spoke, but I let my mind wander off as I dunked my head under the water.

The warm water was like a cocoon, secure, safe and isolated from everything that could hurt me. I didn't have to worry about my heart breaking into a million little pieces when I left. I didn't have to worry about hurting Kail. I wasn't overwhelmed with the emotions he stirred in me. I could simply float in the warm water and silence and it would be like it always had been; quiet, alone, safe.

I don't know how long I was locked inside my mind floating in the water. It felt like mere moments, but suddenly Lex was holding my shoulders firmly and shaking me, "Are you okay? Mel! Answer me!"

I blinked and nodded my head, "I'm okay. Sorry. I was lost in thought," my voice sounded soft and far away.

Lex hopped out of the hot tub and held open a robe, "Too much heat maybe, come on, get out and we'll head inside."

She wrapped me up in the robe and guided me into the house. She led me through the kitchen, up the stairs and into my bedroom.

She let go of me and pulled back the covers of the bed. I had started shivering as soon as she had let go of my hand. She guided me into the bed and tucked me in under the big comforter. Then she climbed onto the bed and staying on top of the covers she curled up next to me, "How are you feeling?" she asked softly.

"Confused," I whispered.

"Confused about what?" she asked as she moved a lock of my hair off my face. A single tear rolled down my cheek as I thought about Kail asleep in the next room. Lex noticed and made the connection, "Oh," she whispered with a tone of sadness in her voice.

We stayed there silent and still for a few minutes until I found my voice, "I want to see where things go…but I am so afraid. Under the water it was so warm and I was so alone, like I had always been, it felt safe. It felt safer than loving someone."

Lex ran her fingers through my hair and it made me feel like a small child being comforted after a nightmare, "I know it feels safe to lock yourself up inside, and in a way it is safe. If you never open yourself up, there's no risk of being hurt."

I nodded my head in agreement and felt a couple more tears spill down my face.

"But when you open yourself up, you give yourself the chance to feel so much more than just hurt. You give yourself the chance to feel joy, happiness, love, bliss, pleasure and peace. Kail has never made you feel scared, you make yourself feel scared. Let him make you feel how he makes you feel and focus on that. It's okay to be happy, even if it doesn't last forever."

I let out a breath I hadn't realized I had been holding. I whispered, "I'll try," as my eyes fluttered closed. Within moments I was fast asleep.

The smell of coffee and cinnamon buns brought me out of a dream where I was surrounded by flower petals and water.

I had that moment of panic where you wake up and aren't sure where you are. Then my eyes found Kail trying to balance a tray and close the door at the same time. I smiled and sat up in bed.

He came over to me with a tray ready of coffee and cinnamon buns that were still steaming from the oven and gooey with icing. There was also a single lily on the tray; my favorite flower.

"For the rest of the world, it's almost dinner time. For someone who had an adventure in the middle of the night and is just now waking up, it's breakfast. So I figured I would bring you a little something. How are you feeling?"

"I'm okay, just tired. Did you say dinner time!?" I took a sip of coffee and sighed as its warmth filled me.

"Ya, it's just after seven at night...and that is decaf," Kail said as he put his hand to my forehead like he was checking my temperature. "You should eat a bun. I brought up a couple, but there's more downstairs if you feel up to eating a little more," he said with concern in his voice.

"Thanks, but why do you sound all worried?" I asked as I reached for a cinnamon bun.

I hadn't felt hungry but they smelled good and I wanted to make him feel better so I took a bite. As I chewed I suddenly felt like I hadn't eaten in days and could have eaten the whole batch of buns. Instead I just ate the two he had brought up.

"Lex left a note for Kass telling her about you being up in the night and going to the hot tub and getting overheated. We've been taking turns checking on you every hour since we found out. We were giving you one more hour and then forcing you awake and taking you to the hospital."

I licked my fingers as I finished the last cinnamon bun, "That's sweet of you guys, but it's just a little heat exhaustion. Rest and I'll be fine. And more of these, they are delicious!"

Kail laughed and kissed my forehead tenderly, "I'm happy to see your doing okay. I'll go grab you some more. How about some bacon?"

I looked up at him with longing in my eyes and the coffee cup halfway to my lips. He just laughed and said, "Bacon too," as he headed back downstairs.

I mulled over what had happened with Lex as I ate my breakfast in bed for dinner and Kail lay next to me reading one of his text books. I was still terrified, but I knew I couldn't lock myself away after having felt so much. I would just have to wait and see where life led me.

By the time I had polished off a serving of bacon and a couple more cinnamon buns I was overcome with exhaustion, "Thank you so much for being so sweet and taking such good care of me and bringing me dinner breakfast in bed. I really am touched…and I'm also exhausted and now I just want to sleep again, but I feel like that's selfish after you have done so much for me," I said as I blinked to keep my eyes focused.

Kail put his hand to my forehead again, "Don't you dare worry about me right now. You just take care of you and I will too. How about we clear this stuff up and you rest some more?"

He cleared the tray away, tucked the sheets in snug around me and then sat down on the bed beside me on top of the covers. He caressed my face gently, then kissed my forehead and said, "You rest and get better and I will see you tomorrow."

As he was moving to get out of the bed I grabbed his wrist and pulled him to me, "Please, stay with me," I whispered.

I fell asleep with his strong arms holding me tight, his body giving me warmth, and I was happy and content.

I had reflected thought, considered alternatives and fallen down the rabbit hole. In Kail's arms it all felt right. I had no idea what would happen between us. I was clueless as to how we could possibly make this last. I just knew that it felt like the truth, and that was a good thing.

NOVEMBER 15

When I woke up, the bed was empty.

Before Kail I had never slept through the night with anyone. Yet in a short period of time I had become so used to it that it felt strange and wrong not to have him there at my side as I woke up. The bed felt empty and cold without him beside me.

Then the events of the last couple days went flying through my head and suddenly I was grateful that he wasn't beside me.

It's not as if we were a couple. We both knew I had to go back to Montana soon and neither of us had broached the subject of what would happen between us when I went back.

And if I was honest with myself, I didn't want to go back. I couldn't bear that idea of not being with him.

I felt tears well up in my eyes as the overwhelming emotions crashed around inside me. Then I saw my laptop and I reached for it like a lifeline.

~ Seize the initiative today. If you don't you will look back and wonder what might have been. So do something daring! ~

Seizing the initiative was terrifying…but I had already come so far, what was one more terrifying act?

An hour later I was showered and sipping coffee as Kass asked me over and over again how I was feeling.

"I'm fine, honest. I feel as good as new. I just needed some rest. Where's Kail?"

"He's at school. He stayed home from classes yesterday to take care of you, so he ran over to meet with his study partners and find out what he missed. He should be back soon. Are you sure you are okay? You don't seem like yourself?"

It was clear that Kass was still concerned, and that was sweet, but what was plaguing me now was not a physical illness that could be cured. There was nothing she could do to help ease this pain inside my chest, "I'm still a little tired and there's something I wanted to talk to Kail about, that's all."

The look she gave me said that she did not believe a word I was saying, but that she would not push the issue just yet. I gave a small smile of thanks and she patted my shoulder gently, "If there's anything I can do, just let me know. Kail should be home soon and I have some scrapbooking I was hoping to catch up on today. So I'll be in my craft room if you need me for anything," she gave my shoulder a small squeeze as she got up to leave.

"Kass," I called out to her as she was about to leave the kitchen. She turned to look at me and I could see sadness in her eyes, "Thank you; for everything. For being my friend all this time, for welcoming me into your home, for giving me so many experiences I could have never had without you, and for encouraging and supporting me to find myself. That's what this trip has all been about, and I have found more than I could have ever imagined."

She smiled at me sweetly, "You are very welcome, for everything," and she left the room.

I sat in the living room attempting to read for about an hour. I had spent the past twenty minutes trying to read the same page over and over again, but none of it seemed to register. I was too focused on listening for the sound of Kail coming home.

When I did hear him arrive, I ran to the door to meet him. He seemed surprised and happy to see me, which only made my heart hurt more. "I need to talk to you, upstairs," I said solemnly and then headed up to my room.

Kail followed, as I knew he would. He sat down on the bed next to me, put his arm around me, hugged me tight and whispered, "What's wrong?"

Seize the initiative. Jump right in, for better or worse...

"I've been thinking a lot the last couple days about how I'm feeling about stuff and I've been struggling with it. So I need to get a couple things out in the open."

Kail just sat there looking at me with his big blue eyes, taking in everything I was saying and waiting for me to unburden myself.

I took a deep breath and pushed forward, "I know we both know this, but I want to make sure it's clear...I'm going back to Montana soon...another week or so probably."

Kail nodded his head yes and I thought I saw something flash through his eyes, but he said nothing.

"I've never been in a situation like this before. I have no idea what the protocol is or how I'm supposed to feel or act. All I know is that I'm torn between wanting to spend as much time with you as possible before I leave; and avoiding you at all costs until I leave so that leaving won't be so hard," my voice caught in my throat on the last word and I felt the tears welling up in my eyes.

Kail cupped my cheek in his hand and said in a soft voice, "I don't know what the protocol here is either. I'm just doing what feels right, and what feels right to me is being with you. I know you have to go back soon and I hope to spend as much time together as we can before you leave. I know it'll be hard when you go back, but I'd rather have another week of happiness before you leave than be even more miserable when you leave."

I was speechless as a couple tears rolled down my cheeks. Kail brushed them away with this thumb and then gently kissed me. At the touch of his lips all my fears seemed to vanish and all that mattered was that we were together here and now. I wrapped my arms around him and held him close as our lips found each other with a tenderness I had never felt before.

We spent the next few hours lying in bed talking and cuddling. It was blissful.

Then there was a knock on my door, "Hey you two horn dogs, dinner is almost ready so put some clothes on!"

It was Lex's voice.

I hadn't known she was coming over. I jumped out of bed and ran into my closet. I pulled on a pair of black leggings and a dark green crochet style sweater. My hair was fluffy and tousled and I was completely natural with no makeup. I looked in the mirror and I felt pretty, sexy and confident for the first time in my life.

Kail had pulled his jeans and t-shirt back on and we headed down to the kitchen.

Lex was standing at the counter putting dinner rolls into a basket. As always, she stood out and drew my eyes to her. Today her hair was pulled back into a pony tail and she was wearing red and black plaid leggings with a black miniskirt and a black tank top that said in bold red writing, "I don't have to outrun the zombies…I just have to outrun you" She had black eye liner and sheer lip gloss. She looked natural and wild all at the same time. I would never understand how she pulled that look off.

We all sat, ate, talked, laughed and had a good meal together. Even Liam had gotten home from work in time to join us. It was a wonderful meal and truly felt like a family dinner, even though I was not a part of this family by blood.

After dinner Liam announced that he was taking Kass out for desert. Kail looked at me and smiled, "I have some homework to do too. I had best get started," and he bounded up the stairs. I knew he wanted me to follow him so we could do what Lex had accused us of earlier, but I wanted to talk to Lex first.

I told Kass we would clean up from dinner and watches as she and Liam left.

"So how're you feeling about things today?" Lex asked once we were alone.

I smiled as I loaded the dishwasher, "Better. I talked to Kail a bit today about my having to go back home and I feel a bit better about it all. I'm still terrified of hurting him and being hurt myself…but I'm focussing on the now and trying not to worry about the then."

Suddenly Lex was hugging me tightly, "Yay!" she shouted as she squeezed me. When she let me go she had a big smile on her face, "I know I don't know Kail from anyone and we hardly know each other, but I am just so happy for you two! You're just so darn cute together!"

Lex's enthusiasm was contagious and I was filled with a sense of calm and joy as we finished cleaning up from dinner.

With the kitchen all cleaned up Lex grabbed her bag and walked past me to the bathroom, "I brought my swimsuit this time. I'm heading out to the hot tub so you two have the house to yourselves. Have fun!"

I ran up the stairs, taking them two at a time, and burst into his room. He was sitting on his bed with his laptop beside him and a text book in his lap. He looked up at me with a started expression.

I pulled my clothes off as I walked over to the bed. I tossed his book on the floor and put his laptop under the bed, "Take your clothes off," I said in a stern voice.

I crawled onto the bed beside him as he stared at me dumbfounded, "Melina, what's going on?" he asked, clearly confused and a little nervous about how aggressive I was being.

I tugged on his belt loop and said, "Now!" and he could see the determination in my eyes. He quickly threw his clothes on the floor, and then looked at me with a somewhat apprehensive expression on his face.

It was sex on a scale I had never before experienced. When it was over we lay tangled together covered in sweat and breathing heavy.

After a few moments to catch our breath Kail kissed my forehead, "Not that I didn't enjoy myself…but what was all that about?"

"Kass and Liam were gone and Lex went out to the hot tub so we had the house to ourselves for about twenty minutes. I wanted to take advantage of the privacy," I said with a mischievous grin.

"Ahhh…so that's why you tried to rape me and now look like the cat that ate the canary?"

I nodded my head yes as I snuggled against him. We lay there like that for a while; neither of us saying anything, just holding each other close.

Then I heard the garage door open and close. I threw on boxers and a tank top and headed down to see how the rest of Kass's night was.

Liam's idea of desert had been to take Kass to Tiffany's and buy her a new charm for her growing collection of charm bracelets. This one was a white and yellow gold daisy with a diamond in the middle. On the back he had it engraved to say "M.R. 2012" to commemorate my trip out here.

Of course she was glowing and couldn't keep her hands off him. I would never say that Kass married Liam for his money because I knew how much she genuinely loved him. The money was just a few hundred thousand pounds of icing on top of the cake; and Kass never said no to icing.

She showed off her new charm, which led to showing off all of her charm bracelets. In their years together she had twelve complete bracelets and was working on numbers thirteen and fourteen simultaneously. One was in honor of their relationship and one was just about her.

It all seemed very pointless to me, but it made her happy, so who was I to judge.

After an hour of looking at charm bracelets and hearing how wonderful Liam was, I'd had enough. I said goodnight and headed back up to Kail's room.

I found him lying in his bed, his text book open on the pillow next to him and a little bit of drool on his pillow. He was drooling and snoring and yet somehow I still found it adorable. The thought frightened me a little, but then he whispered my name in his sleep and I melted inside as my fears washed away.

I climbed into bed next to him and savored the feeling of having him next to me. I took a deep breath and reminded myself that right now, this was all that mattered, everything else I would deal with when the time came.

NOVEMBER 16

When I woke up I was in Kail's bed alone. His side of the bed was cold and the blankets were tangled around my legs. I guessed he had been out of bed for a half hour or more. But he never said goodbye. He had left for classes while I had been sleeping before, but he always gave me a kiss and said goodbye before he left.

His alarm clock said it was just after nine. I laid there for a few minutes thinking about the fact that he hadn't said anything before he left. It made me want to curl up in a ball and cry. It made me feel like this was more to me than it was to him.

As I tried to tell myself it wasn't a big deal that he had left without saying goodbye, I started to drift back to sleep.

Just as sleep was about to envelop me I felt his lips, warm and gentle on my forehead, "Goodbye, have a good day," he whispered softly before he snuck out of the room. I let out a sigh of relief;; he must have been in the bathroom getting ready.

Seeing him always made me smile and make my heart beat a little faster. When I thought he had left without saying goodbye and then he showed up unexpectedly, I felt as if my whole heart were going to explode out of my chest.

I felt giddy and light headed afterward, like I was a little drunk or high. I could still feel his lips on my forehead even though it had happened minutes ago. I felt as if I could feel his lips on me forever, and still not get enough.

I laid there smiling that dopey smile that says you are falling in love; the smile that tells the world that you are under the influence and should not be operating heavy machinery. Love really is like a drug. It impairs your judgment, makes you do things you wouldn't normally do, and it makes you happy about doing them.

As soon as I realized I was tossing the word 'love' around in my head, I froze.

Love!? I had only known this guy for a couple weeks; I could not possibly love him! I was not one of those girls who fell in love with every guy who gave them a 'Hey baby, how you doin?' grin and thrust his hips in her direction. I was a logical, rational woman who made choices with her head.

But what about my heart? I had never made a decision with my heart until I decided to take this trip. Before this, decisions were always made rationally and methodically and emotion had nothing to do with it.

But making an emotional decision to travel from Montana to Texas to visit a friend was vastly different than falling in love with that friend's brother.

Clearly this issue was far beyond my realm of experience or expertise. I needed help and guidance.

I wrapped the sheet around myself and headed into my room to check my scope.

~ You are going to have to make some big decisions. You will make them with ease. You should have been this decisive earlier ~

Big decisions…nail on the head.

Kail is a great guy, he is sweet, funny, kind, smart, understanding, generous, accepting, supportive and a great

Mariya Taylor

lover. But he is also younger than me, still figuring his life out, and above all…he lives over one thousand and five hundred miles away from me.

I had never been able to make an in the flesh relationship work, how on earth would I make a long distance one work? Kail obviously needed to stay here to finish his degree, but then what? I have my job back home and he has his dreams of owning his own company here. One of us would have to move, or we both would. It was too much to ask of someone; so how I felt didn't matter.

I had been struggling with all of this for days and every time I thought I had made my mind up to live in the moment and enjoy whatever we had while it lasted; I'd be wracked with anxiety again. When I was in his arms, it all seemed worth whatever pain might happen later.

But when we were apart, it seemed so terrifying. I couldn't keep living on this rollercoaster of emotions. My scope was right; I needed to make a decision.

With my mind made up on a course of action I headed back into Kail's room to grab my clothes from the night before. In my search around his room I stepped on one of his shirts and when I bent down to pick it up I caught a whiff of his cologne. My eyes fluttered and I smiled like an idiot as my heart did uncoordinated jumping jacks in my chest.

If just the smell of him got this reaction there was no way I could be around him for the rest of my time here and act like it was okay that I would be leaving soon. I was in big trouble. I needed time to think and sort things out. I needed time to process and do some logical risk analysis.

I threw on a pair of jeans and a teal blouse, ran a brush through my hair, splashed water on my face, gargled with mouthwash and ran down into the kitchen.

As I had expected, Kass was sitting at the table sipping coffee and working on her laptop, "Good mornin darlin," she said in a cheerful affected southern drawl.

"Morning. I was wondering if you had plans today?" I said in a rush. Kass looked at me, the look that said she knew something was up and wanted to ask but was too much of a lady to do it and was kicking herself for it.

"Not a thing. Why do you ask?" her voice was overly sweet and I knew she was dying to know what was going on.

"I need to relax a little. I was thinking I could treat us to a spa day maybe? Get massages and mud wraps and facials and all that jazz. What do you think?"

She eyed me suspiciously, but I knew I had her at the word 'spa'. Sure enough in another moment her face lit up and she bounded up out of her chair, "Sounds delightful! Let me go throw on some clothes!"

Three hours later my body was a relaxed, exfoliated, moisturized blob of jelly. Unfortunately my heart was in a state of panic and shock and my mind remained conflicted and frantic.

Kass and I had driven to her favorite spa and enjoyed a long, hot mud wrap, then an hour long full body massage, followed by a facial from a very attractive young man. I was currently soaking my feet in warm water as a young woman showed me a variety of polish colors.

I was so wrapped up in my own thoughts I didn't even pay attention and waved my hand at random to select a color.

I loved every moment of being here. I felt like for the first time in my life I was really being me. Not who anyone else wanted me to be, not who I thought I should be, but just me. It felt liberating and exhilarating…and terrifying.

Back home I might not have been the real me, but I knew my place. I knew what was expected of me, I knew where I was heading, and I knew where I stood and what I felt.

Here, it was like everything was upside down and sideways. I had no idea what was expected of me or what would happen next or even what I wanted to happen next. So much was happening so fast. My life was usually calm and whenever something did happen, it happened slowly.

This pace of life and these events were far beyond anything I had ever experienced or expected. I was enjoying the ride, but felt so drastically out of my element.

I had to think about what would happen when I left. Going from my life there to here was remarkable and exciting. To leave all of this and go back to my life there seemed so depressing and empty. I felt like the longer I stayed here the harder going back to Montana would be.

The idea of going back to Montana so soon filled me with a sadness I had no name for. It was as if my heart had simply lost the will to continue beating in my chest and all the color and sound drained out of the world until I was left in a void of black and white silence.

Then the young woman who had been painting my toes gently tapped the top of my foot to tell me she was done and I was snapped back to bright, vivid, noisy Texas.

Just like my toes.

It seemed while I was lost in my own little world I had waved ambiguously at a bright, vivid, noisy shade of neon green.

Just like my recent actions, my toe nails were not at all like the me I had been for the first twenty nine years of my life. Perhaps I was finding my true self here…or perhaps I had left my true self behind in Montana.

There was only one way to find out. I needed to go back home.

For all of my certainty that going back home was the most logical, safe choice…I couldn't bring myself to tell anyone.

Kass and I went home and cooked dinner together and I couldn't tell her. We ate dinner with Kail and I couldn't tell him. The three of us played some games on the Wii and I couldn't tell them.

I went to bed around nine claiming I had a headache. For the second night since Kail and I had shared that night in the hotel, I slept alone. The bed felt huge and empty and I had restless dreams about airplanes crashing. Every time I would fall asleep I would see a plane flying peacefully through the clouds, then suddenly it would start to plummet. It would nose dive for the ground and just before it hit, I would wake up in a cold sweat.

NOVEMBER 17

I had the airplane crashing dream six times during the night. Come seven in the morning I was fed up. If I couldn't get a decent sleep, than I might as well start this day and get it over with.

I knew Kass would fight me on going home early. I half hoped Kail would too. I wasn't sure about Lex.

I had a quick shower and threw on a pair of jeans and a long sleeved burgundy blouse and headed for the kitchen.

Sure enough, Kass and Liam were having coffee and munching on bagels while they shared the paper. Kass was resting her head on Liam's shoulder as she read an article. He was gently stroking her hair as he read the same one.

They were so sweet and adorable and looking at them made my heart hurt. I wanted that with someone. I wanted to wake up with someone every morning. I wanted to share breakfast and the paper on weekends and be sweet and loving long after we were married. I wanted love, romance, intimacy and tenderness in my life.

I had those things here…with Kail. Back home there was only solitude and isolation.

In my moment of reflection Kass noticed me, "Sweetie? Are you okay?"

I shook my head to clear it as she walked towards me. She put her hand on my shoulder and I could see the concern in her eyes.

I opened my mouth to speak, but no words came out. Suddenly I was crying, Kass was holding me and trying to comfort me and Liam was trying to escape from the kitchen, which had unexpectedly turned into a boiling cauldron of female emotion.

After about ten minutes of crying and sobbing while Kass stroked my hair, I was finally calming down a little bit. I let her lead me into the living room to sit down and when she asked if I could talk I nodded my head yes.

She started rubbing my back as I struggled to find the words.

"Yesterday I thought a lot about things and decided I should go back home. I had awful dreams all night about a plane crash, that's why I'm up so early. I came down to talk to you about going home and I saw you and Liam and you were just so sweet and cute and in love and I…" I started to cry again.

Kass rubbed my back and said soft encouraging words until I could choke out, "I want what you two have and there's nothing for me back home. But here…here Kail makes me feel like one day maybe we could have that; but I don't even know what we are and I have to go back home eventually and what then!?"

I exasperatedly threw my head in my hands and started sobbing again.

Kass gave me a minute and then she said softly, "Thanks to you I am actually starting to get to know my brother for the first time in my life. I don't claim to be an expert on him or men in general…but I think he has fallen for you. I think if you asked him to go to Montana he would. You two could make a go of it."

I flung my head up and wailed, "No!" I shook my head emphatically, "he needs to finish his school…after that…I couldn't. I couldn't ask him to leave his friends and family and his dreams of starting his own company here."

Kass rubbed my back as my tears flowed. After a few minutes she said softly, almost hesitantly, "I have been thinking that you could always move here. Liam could get you a job at his company, they are always hiring people, and you could live here with us until you saved up enough for a place of your own. Then you and Kail could see how things go and there wouldn't be this unspoken time limit on things pressuring you both."

As I let the idea sink in my tears dried up. My first thought was that I had ties back home. I had a job, an apartment, my family.

But I could go back home and give my notice at work. My lease was month to month. And my family…what I felt was a sense of obligation, not any actual affection or desire to be near them. It was clear that I was better off without them and I suspected they were doing just fine without me.

Maybe I could move here. It hadn't occurred to me, but it certainly sounded plausible. Just having the idea in my head as an option suddenly made everything feel better. Now things with Kail didn't seem as terrifying and overwhelming.

"That might actually work," I said in a soft voice.

Kass smiled, "I know, I've been planning it for days!" she laughed and it was contagious. "Feeling better now?" she asked as she patted my shoulder. I nodded my head yes as I played the idea over and over in my head. "Good. Now

I'd better go tell Liam that the crying has stopped or he'll barricade himself in our room all day just to be safe."

My stomach grumbled and reminded me that I had not yet had coffee, breakfast or checked my scope. My whole night had been thrown off by the bad dreams and my whole morning had been thrown off by my emotions. Time to get things back on track!

I grabbed my laptop and set up at the kitchen table with a coffee, bagel and some fruit and checked my scope.

   ~ Give yourself permission to dream big. The only impossible things in life are the ones you give up on.~

I sat at the table basking in the early morning sunshine as I ate my breakfast and imagined a future where I could live close to the only real friend I'd ever had, where I could have a job I was proud of and could advance in, and where I might finally find love.

An hour later I crept into Kail's room, stripped off my clothes and quietly crawled into bed next to him. In his sleep he mumbled something incoherent and snuggled next to me, putting his arm around me and holding me close.

He was so warm and strong. The feeling of his arm around me made me feel safe and protected. The roughness of his beard as it rubbed against my shoulder made me smile. He was so uniquely HIM and somehow he wanted me. It blew my mind and filled my heart in a way I could have never imagined.

I cuddled into him more and let myself drift into a fantasy dream land where we lived in the same city and could follow these feelings growing between us; where we had a chance to be a real couple, to live together, to get married, and to live happily ever after.

My mind was miles away contemplating the perfect future when Kail woke up. I felt his arm around me stiffen and heard his breathing change and I knew he was awake. I turned in his arms and I kissed the tip of his nose as his eyes fluttered open, "Good morning sleepy head."

"Well good morning to you too. Last I checked you wanted to sleep alone and seemed to be thinking very serious things. Then I wake up with you naked in my bed being cute. What changed?"

I gave his nose another quick peck to let him know things were okay, "I didn't sleep well. When I got up Kass and I had a big talk and she pointed out some options I hadn't considered. Things are still complicated and uncertain, butnow I feel like there are more possibilities. Then I came up here and got into bed waiting for you to wake up."

We lay in bed for hours talking about everything from philosophy to zombies and I felt so at peace and contented; it was as if the rest of the world, with all its hardships and suffering, didn't exist.

At a lull in the conversation as we held each other close, I was overwhelmed by how lucky I was to have this moment. I was filled with so much love and emotion that I couldn't contain it and I started to cry.

He held me as I cried. He stroked my hair and kissed my forehead and just let me cry. He didn't make false promises or try to stop my tears. He didn't ask me if I was okay or try to distract me. He just held me and cared for me and gave me a safe place to pour my heart out.

When my tears had finally dried up and I could speak I looked up at him and smiled, "Thank you," I whispered in a voice grown hoarse.

He squeezed me tightly and kissed my forehead, "Your welcome. Feel like telling me what's wrong now?"

"Nothing is wrong. Everything is very, very right. It's just a lot and it's overwhelming. I feel like I don't deserve everything wonderful that has happened to me."

The tears were welling up in my eyes again, but Kail stopped them with a kiss. He held my face in his hands and I was swept up in his blue eyes that made me feel as if I were drowning in a sea of hope.

"You deserve everything that is good and right. You deserve all the happiness and joy its possible for one person to feel. You deserve so much more than you have been given in life. You have been brainwashed to think you are unworthy and ugly…but you are remarkable, beautiful, amazing and wonderful. You can do anything you want and you deserve even more."

Before I could protest, he silenced me with another kiss that melted what was left of my fears.

I had planned to cuddle with Kail for a bit then shower and head downstairs to see how Kass was doing.

Instead, Kail and I fell asleep and woke up to Lex knocking on the door and hollering, "Time to stop humping and come down for dinner you two wild bunnies!"

I was instantly awake and frantic, filled with the adrenaline rush of having slept in past your alarm. I threw on clothes I had scattered around Kail's room and headed downstairs.

While dinner was delicious - roast chicken, potatoes, vegetables and homemade biscuits – I hardly tasted any of it.

My mind was far away, considering the options of moving here. How would I leave my job? How would I tell my parents? How would I get all my stuff here?

I was off in my own little dreamland when I felt Kail's hands on my shoulders, "Dinner is done. Why don't we go out for a walk?"

I smiled up at him and followed him outside into the brisk November air.

We walked along the sidewalks hand in hand. We didn't speak, but we didn't need to. We were both busy soaking in the crisp, clean air, the stars in the sky and out hands entwined together.

After an hour of aimless wandering around Kass's suburb, we walked back into the house to find it silent and dark. We headed upstairs to Kail's room in silence so as not to wake anyone. We undressed, climbed into bed and fell asleep holding each other close.

NOVEMBER 18

I woke up slowly and languidly. I stretched like a cat and reached over to cuddle, and found myself alone in bed.

Somehow even though I had the affection of an amazing man, waking up in my bed alone brought tears to my eyes and left me feeling alone and empty.

I glanced at the clock and saw that it was getting close to ten. I guessed that everyone would have been up ages ago and I was the last one still in bed. I took a deep breath and resolved not to allow the happiness and joy of last night to be eclipsed by the gloom of waking up alone.

Looking for a little cosmic validation I turned on my computer to check my scope.

~ Don't lock up your emotions today. Confide in your loved ones and they will guide you on the path to your dreams ~

Well if that wasn't as clear as sunshine on a cloudy day, I didn't know what was.

I threw on my nightshirt and headed to the kitchen. I walked in to find Kail unloading the dishwasher. I ran up to him and hugged him tightly.

He chuckled at my enthusiasm and moved his laptop off the bed, "Well good morning. I take it you slept well?"

I nodded my head, "I slept well enough, but waking up alone was hard. I've gotten used to waking up with you beside me."

Kail kissed the top of my head and squeezed me tightly, "I'm sorry. You seemed so peaceful; I didn't want to wake you. I was making coffee to bring up to you," he said gesturing to the percolating coffee.

Suddenly I felt silly for being upset. He was so sweet and thoughtful and I had been selfish expecting him to always stay in bed with me until I was ready to get up.

I leaned in and kissed him passionately and he pulled away from me surprised at the sudden change. I smiled up at him, "I am a woman with emotions like the ocean. Deep and strong, but with swiftly shifting tides. I was overreacting. I can't find words to say how amazing you are or how thankful I am to you for everything you have shown me and given me. I want to show you," I slipped my fingers under the waistband of his boxer briefs and grinned up at him.

He smiled down at me and said, "I don't always understand how you get from point A to point B…but point B often seems to involve you removing my underwear so I'm not going to pick at it too much," as he let me lead him upstairs.

Once we were in his room I drowned myself in his kisses and breathed in the scent of him as deeply as I could and tried to show him with my touch and kiss just how much he meant to me.

It was hours later when we made our way back down to the kitchen. Kass was mixing up a batch of biscuits for dinner and grinned at us, "I see you two found each other before you finished making the coffee. It's a little late now; but there are some leftovers from dinner in the fridge for lunch if you'd like."

Her ability to adjust to things never ceased to amaze me. I had no siblings, but I imagined if I did that it would be strange for me to have them hooking up with a close friend under my roof, but she didn't seem fazed by it at all. It was all too strange for me to completely comprehend, but it seemed somehow perfectly normal to her.

Kail and I ate lunch in silence. We may not have said any words, but anyone looking at us would have been sickened by the sweetness as we sat shoulder to shoulder making eye constant, smiling and kissing as we ate. Kass kept working on her biscuits humming pleasantly to herself, letting us have this simple moment together.

After a lazy evening around the house playing video games and helping Kass make yet another delicious meal - this time it was ribs, roasted potatoes, corn on the cob and her delicious biscuits - Kail and I went to bed early. We slept in my room so he could leave for class and I could keep sleeping in my own bed.

I fell asleep surrounded by the warmth of his body, wrapped in his arms and feeling so safe, contented and treasured.

NOVEMBER 19

While my body was lying safe and warm next to Kail, my mind wandered into the world of dreams as I slept. In my dream world I was neither safe nor warm. I was leaving.

I saw Kass pull up to the airport with sadness on her face. I saw Kail and I in the backseat holding hands, both too afraid to look at each other for fear it would be too painful. I saw Lex in the front seat looking awkward and uncomfortable.

We all piled out of the car and silently headed to my departure gate - I was certain it was a dream because there was no luggage to check, lines to wait in or security clearance.

Kass hugged me and said, "Have a safe trip home."

Kail hugged me and said, "It was fun. I wish you all the best."

Lex hugged me and said, "Thanks for shaking us up a bit."

The three of them stood ten feet away from me, but it might as well have been the Grand Canyon separating us. And that canyon was filled with all of the things we weren't saying to each other and all of the feelings we weren't expressing. In my dream we just stayed there, frozen like a tableau of indecision, inaction and pain; until Kail kissed my forehead and pulled me out of the horrible dream.

"I have to leave for class. Have a good day and I'll be home this afternoon. Go back to sleep," he whispered before kissing my lips softly and leaving the room.

I laid there, alone in the early morning glow, and I felt so full of emotions, thoughts and hopes. The dream terrified me. The idea of leaving with so many things unsaid and emotions unexpressed made me feel cold inside. I couldn't let that happen, but I wasn't sure how to avoid it. After all, I was only one person, I had no control over what anyone else said, did or felt.

In hopes of yet another inspirational message from the universe, I checked my scope.

> *~ Let your heart speak truthfully and without censorship today. Your words will free you and compel others to do the same ~*

I had no idea what I would say, but I knew I needed to take yet another big risk and get it all out in the open before it was too late. I had to talk to Kass, Kail and Lex about how I felt and ask them to share how they felt. I had to trust they would all be open and honest with me in return. The idea of opening up so much was terrifying, but I knew in my heart it was what had to happen.

I showered and pulled on a pair of yoga pants and the t-shirt with the tree on it. If I was going to face the challenge of opening up my heart to people who had the power to crush it, I was going to be comfortable.

I grabbed my laptop and headed to the kitchen, where I munched on a bagel and surfed the net while I waited for Kass to get up.

When she walked in she smiled and opened her mouth, no doubt to wish me a good morning, but I cut her off, "I need to say something and I need you to listen. Is that okay?"

I watched as a million thoughts ran through her mind about what I was about to say. Perhaps one of them was close to accurate, but chances were high that they were all far worse than anything I was about to say.

I took a deep breath and jumped in before I could chicken out, "I have decided that I need to head home soon. I haven't looked at flights yet, but I figure within the next week I should head back. As much as I would love to make this vacation last a lifetime, I have to return to the real world eventually. I need you to know that your friendship has meant so much to me over the past couple years. I never thought I would ever actually meet you face to face or that our friendship could get any stronger or deeper than it was before I came here. A month ago our friendship was the most meaningful one I'd had in my entire life. I was completely happy and content in that friendship. Then I came here and our friendship exploded. I can never thank you enough for your friendship, support, advice, encouragement, acceptance and for opening your home up to me. You have shown me the kind of friendship I thought only existed in movies. I only hope I can return even half of the friendship you have given me."

Kass had tears in her eyes that she blinked away as she gave me a huge bear hug, "Sweetie, you're the best!" was all she said as she hugged me and a little of the weight that had been on my shoulders since my dream eased.

I waited until noon to try calling Lex. On the third ring, just as I was certain her voicemail was about to pick up, she answered, "Hi-low, Lex's house of pancakes, can I take your order?"

I couldn't help it, I giggled and felt some of my anxiety ease, "Hey, it's Melina. Thanks, I've already had breakfast…and it's lunch time," I said with a smile on my face.

"Well there's never a bad time for pancakes!" she said with enthusiasm.

"I suppose that's true. Listen, I know this is going to sound kind of nuts…but I had a dream last night that upset me and it involved you a bit so I feel like I need to say something so what happened in my dream doesn't happen in real life. Does that make sense?"

"Oh it makes total sense! Go for it!"

How it could make 'total sense; I didn't know. It sounded insane to me and it was happening inside my head; but she had said go for it, so go for it I went.

"You are unpredictable and that makes me nervous…but you're also an inspiring, vibrant, amazing woman and I am so lucky to have met you and get to know you. So I guess what I'm saying is that I consider you a friend and I hope we'll keep in touch after I leave."

There was a pause, then a deep exhalation, "Oh sweetie you are adorable and thoughtful. Of course we'll keep in touch!.."

I felt more of the weight ease off my shoulders as we talked about my plans for the rest of my time here.

As I hung up the phone I took a slow, deep breath. So far this day was going easier than I had thought it would. But I had saved the biggest and scariest conversation for last. Kail would be home in the next hour or two. I had no idea what I was going to say and I feared that anything I did say would just scare him off or push him away. The thought of losing him brought tears to my eyes in an instant and I had to fight them back.

Love can be liberating and freeing. It can make you feel invincible and on top of the world. It can also make you fear with every fiber of your being. Love is a fragile, delicate, fickle thing. It can be torn away as easily as it can bloom. To love is to put yourself at risk for the most gut wrenching pain a person can feel - the pain of having that which you love taken from you.

I was staring into that abyss now, and the abyss stared back with cold, unblinking eyes as my fear grew.

I distracted myself with laundry and video games until I heard him come into the house. I froze for a second. Then I heard him fumbling around in the laundry room that attached the garage to the house. He laughed, a deep, rich, masculine laugh that melted my fears and made me ache to hold him.

He came out of the laundry room carrying a pair of my panties with a big smile on his face.

They were a pair of boyshort panties that said, "Naughty or Nice" on the front and had a bull's-eye on the back saying, "I'll pay the price". I hadn't understood why they were amusing when Kass insisted I buy them. She had to explain to me the implication that being naughty meant you got a spanking. Then she had to explain to me that some people found that arousing. She thought my ignorance was endearing and adorable. I had felt like the biggest loser in the world.

Seeing Kail holding the panties I had tried to avoid him seeing me wear, I started blushing furiously. As soon as he saw me blushing he laughed even harder and came to sit beside me. He put his arm around me and pulled me into him and whispered in my ear, "Have you been naughty or nice?"

I hadn't thought it was possible to blush more than I already was.

I was wrong.

My face lit up like a house on fire and I couldn't didn't dare look up at him as I said in a voice gone soft and quivery with embarrassment, "I need to talk to you about something. Can we go up to your room?"

He gave my shoulder a squeeze, "Sure thing; lead the way."

I stood up and started walking towards the stairs as Kail came up behind me and smacked my ass.

I let out a girly squeal of shock, which made him laugh that rich masculine laugh again. I had to admit that aside from surprising me, I had also felt a jolt of electricity run through me with the smack. Perhaps if this conversation went well, someday we could test those waters.

We got into Kail's room and I sat down on the bed with him beside me. I couldn't bring myself to look at him as I let the words flow out of my mouth. Not allowing myself to analyze or dissect what I was saying because I knew if I hesitated for just a second to consider my words that I wouldn't say them at all.

"I came on this vacation looking for an escape, looking for a change, looking for myself. I found all of those things and that has been amazing. But I also found you. I didn't have much relationship experience, but I had a little and I thought I knew what it was all about. I was wrong. Being with you has shown me that my past relationships were hollow imitations of the real thing. I am going back home within the week, I'm not sure exactly when, but soon. I can't leave without you knowing how I feel. And it's okay if you don't feel the same, I never expected to feel this way and I certainly don't expect you to feel the same. This whole thing was so out of the blue it sort of shook my sense of reality and I forgot to consider that I had to go back home, which is why this is so hard. But I need you to know before I go that…" I paused, my heart catching in my throat, my voice quivering with emotion, my blood thundering through my ears, "I love you," I said in a soft breathy whisper as I fought back tears.

As soon as the words were out of my mouth I was filled with an overwhelming dread of not hearing them back, of him laughing in my face, of having him reject me. I felt the tears burst forth in the breath of silence after I had said those three little words I could never take back.

Then I felt his fingers on my chin, forcing me to turn and face him. When I looked into his face it was serious, yet somehow calm. He held my eyes for a second before he parted his lips to speak. Then he closed his mouth. He did that a few times, making him look like a very serious fish. The thought made me smile and that seemed to break his silence.

"There are so many things I could say, that I want to say, but right now all that matters is that I love you too," then he kissed me so tenderly that my heart, which had climbed into my throat just seconds before, melted into a warm ooziness that ran down my throat and through my whole body.

That night Kail and I made love, relishing in the sight,

sound, taste and feel of each other. We whispered 'I love you' over and over as we rediscovered each other. I fell asleep wrapped in his arms and felt as if suddenly everything in the universe made more sense.

NOVEMBER 20

I woke up when Kail's alarm went off. I snuggled against him and squeezed him hard before I let him get out of bed. I watched as he fumbled around the room trying to get ready while he was still half asleep.

Love hadn't made me blind. I saw his imperfections - like the beginnings of a beer belly and how his hair and beard always looked a little like he'd just been electrocuted. I saw his flaws - like how he was obsessive about his text books being in alphabetical order, even when he put them in his backpack, or how everything in his routine had to happen in just the right sequence. All of those quirks made me love him more. They showed me that he was flawed and a little crazy like me.

I watched him the way a small child watches a magic trick; full of wonder, awe and fascination. This man who was so smart, sweet, funny, caring, kind and all around amazing, this man I had fallen completely and irreparably in love with. Somehow this man loved me.

We kissed goodbye and after he left I pulled out my laptop and sank down from the clouds into reality. I went in search of a cheap flight home that would still give me a few days here.

An hour later I had found an incredible deal to fly home the day after Black Friday for half of what I paid to come out here. It gave me four more days here, including this one. I needed to make the most of those four days and get in as much quality time with people as possible.

Before heading to the shower I checked my scope for the day.

*~ Get out into the world and have a good time. Meet
as many interesting new people as you possibly can ~*

Showered and ready to start my fourth last day in Texas I
headed for the kitchen.

Not surprisingly, Kass sat at the table with her laptop. I
gave her a big hug and said, "I told Kail I loved him and
he said he loved me too and then this morning I booked
my flight home, I have four more days. Let's make the
most of them!"

I sat down beside Kass and when I saw the confusion and
worry on her face my own smile melted, "What? What's
wrong?"

She shook her head and let out a sigh, "I just don't
understand. You told him you love him?" I nodded. "And
he said he loved you too?" I nodded again, "And then this
morning you booked a flight home?" I nodded once more
and she let out an exasperated wail of, "Whyyyyyy?"

It was my turn to look confused, "What do you mean
why?"

She put her hands on my shoulders and looked me in the
eyes, "You love him and he loves you. You two are great
together," her voice was calm and rational as she stated
these miracles like every day statements of fact. Then she
started shaking my shoulders as she yelled out, "so why are
you going back to Montana!?"

I couldn't help but laugh as I untangled myself from her
hands, which were still trying to frantically shake me, "I
love him, and he loves me. It's wonderful and amazing and
miraculous; but he has his life here and I have mine back

in Montana. I have commitments and connections and a life there. I can't just abandon it completely. If nothing else I need to go back home and see how we both feel with some time and space between us. I need to deal with my work, apartment and parents. I need to make sure that reality is on the same page as this fairy tale I have been living here."

Kass twirled a bit of her hair around her finger as she considered this burst of rationality. Finally she looked up at me and said, "Okay. I concede that is a valid argument. But promise me you'll be back again soon. Six months at the most before your back. Deal?"

I laughed and hugged her again, "It's a deal!"

That afternoon Kass and I headed to Southlake Town Square to meet Lex for lunch. The Square is about twenty blocks full of shops and restaurants as well as a movie theater and hotel. It's got just about anything you could possibly want and all the shops looked adorably cozy and welcoming. It felt like something out of a movie to be in a big shopping district full of classy stores with two girlfriends. I never even imagined I would have two friends, let alone do something as normal as have lunch and go shopping with the girls.

We had lunch at a quaint place called Snuffer's, where I tried deep fried pickles for the first time. I expected to hate them, but they were so delicious we ordered a second basket! We all talked and laughed and I felt so 'normal' that I kept pinching myself under the table to make sure it was real.

After lunch we wandered up and down the streets checking out stores at random. We found ourselves in

Coach where Kass was drooling over the new line of purses when a woman's voice behind us said, "Lex…is that you?" Her voice was soft and sultry. The kind of voice that drips with confidence and a hint of seduction with every syllable.

All three of us turned and I saw the woman who matched the voice and I had to blink to make sure she was real. She was tall and made of curves. Her jeans and t-shirt did nothing to hide the graceful and perfectly proportioned curves of her body. Her hair was shoulder length and curly without being frizzy. It was a shade of blond that looked like a sunset and judging from her roots, was completely natural. Her skin was the natural warm golden glow you only get from the sun. With the blond hair and tan skin you expected her to have blue eyes to complete the Arian Sun Goddess look…but her eyes were a deep rich brown that seemed to pull you into her as she looked at you. She wore no makeup and yet had perfect skin. She was completely natural and casual and she was the most beautiful woman I had ever seen.

When she recognized Lex she smiled, and I was blindsided. I had no idea she could get more beautiful, but her smile - full of pure happiness and joy - was literally blinding in its sincerity and beauty.

Lex ran over to her and they hugged. It was one of those long, tight hugs where you can tell they don't want to let each other go. As they reluctantly pulled apart the woman stroked Lex's cheek and we were close enough to hear her whisper, "I've missed you"

They stayed there for a moment, staring at each other, before they became aware of the rest of the world and Lex turned to introduce us, "Dell, you know Kass already, and this is Melina, she's visiting from Montana"

The beauty nodded recognition towards Kass and then put out her hand to me. Her skin felt so soft, and somehow the warmth of her touch gave the impression that she had just come in from sunning herself even though the day was somewhat overcast. I tried to say something kind and polite, but my mouth wouldn't work. I just smiled at her like an idiot.

"I'm sorry, I didn't mean to interrupt your shopping, I just wanted to say hi to Lex," she said politely as she took a small step backwards.

Lex shot Kass a look that clearly said she didn't want this woman to walk away, but she couldn't say anything herself.

Kass smiled and said, "You weren't interrupting anything dear, we were just finishing up and trying to decide what to do next. Lex wanted to stay out but the two of us were thinking of heading back home. Do you think you could keep my little sister-in-law company if we went back home?"

Dell smiled again and said, "I'm pretty sure I can manage that. It was nice seeing you again Kass, nice meeting you Melina," and then Kass rushed me out of the store before anyone could say anything else.

We walked to the car in silence and I was completely confused about what had just happened.

We got to the car and when I tried to ask Kass what had just happened she put her finger to her mouth to hush me while she dialed Liam's cell phone. Her half of the conversation went like this:

"Head's up, we just ran into Dell!"
"I don't think so. We'd been at Southlake Square all

afternoon just wandering aimlessly and then suddenly she was there in Coach!"

"They hugged, she touched Lex's face and said she missed her, and then she made to leave. Lex gave me the look so I made an excuse and we high-tailed it outta' there. She's with her right now."

"Judging from the way she responded to her, I'd say hell yes!"

"I'll wait until tomorrow. I don't want to crowd her or make her feel like we're judging."

"Of course I'm scared! When I am not scared when Dell is involved!? But she's older now and hopefully wiser and she needs to make her own mistakes."

"Okay. I promise. I love you."

She hung up the phone and let out a big sigh, "That woman was Dell, as in Magdellaine, as in Lex's first love. She is the woman who completely captivated her and then squished her like a bug on the bottom of her shoe. Lex is still madly in love with her. She shows up out of the blue now and then, wraps Lex up in her spell and disappears without a reason or warning for an unknown period of time."

It all slowly fit into place. Not just their reactions to each other, but Kass and Liam's reactions. I nodded my head yes to show I understood the situation.

Kass and I spent the rest of the afternoon preparing a delicious meal of spinach and feta stuffed chicken with garlic rice and garden salad. Luckily Liam was home in time to enjoy it. After dinner the four of us played a game of Risk before going our separate ways for bed.

I lay down beside Kail, his arm around me holding me close, the warmth of his body next to mine, and I couldn't get the smile off my face. I had never known happiness like this could even exist, and here I was living it. I had a sense of family and belonging; love that warmed me from the inside out and made me feel cherished; friendship that filled my life with laughter, hugs and acceptance.

I had always been content with my little corner of the world where I kept to myself and so did everyone else. After everything I had experienced in this short time here, I knew I could never be content with that lonely little life ever again. Now I knew how happy I could be, and for the first time in my life I believed in that I was worthy of such happiness.

NOVEMBER 21

I was once again in the car with Kass, Kail and Lex on my way to the airport. This time there were hugs and tears and so much love that the air felt thick with emotion. I got on the plane and in the blink of an eye I was landing in Helena. There were no friends to meet me at the airport. My parents couldn't be bothered. There were no welcome home signs. No hugs. No tears. No sign that I had been missed at all. The only thing the air was thick with was loneliness.

I took a cab to my apartment and found it exactly as I had left it; empty and cold.

Suddenly it was morning and I was on my way to work. I walked into the office and found that somehow I was bigger than everyone else.

Not that I had gained a bunch of weight, but like I was a giant and everyone else was like ants. Their voices came to me as high pitched mumblings. I couldn't understand them and I was afraid to move for fear of squishing someone.

I ran out of the office and up the street to my parents' house. As I stepped inside I found that here too I was a giant among ants. My mother was screaming and flailing her arms around and it sounded like the buzzing of an annoying mosquito. My father sat in his chair watching TV not even noticing my presence.

I felt so confused and alone. I had no one here to comfort me or try to help me understand what was happening. I sat down on the sidewalk and started to cry, wishing I was back in Texas with friends and people who loved and understood me.

That's when I felt Kail's lips on my forehead and heard him whisper, "Have a good day, I'll be home as soon as I can. I love you."

I blinked my eyes open, but it was too late, he had already left the room.

I was still in Texas. It was just a dream.

Afraid to slip back into that horrible dream of giants, ants and loneliness; I tried to resist sleep, but in moments my eyes were closing and I was drifting off again.

Three hours later I awoke with a smile on my face. I couldn't remember what I had dreamed after I had fallen back asleep, but clearly it had been more pleasant than earlier.

I could hear birds outside and the sun was shining. I refused to let the dream I could remember bring me down. I was determined to make every day I left here a positive one.

It's true that Kass's worry over Lex seeing Dell had me worried for her as well, but other than that everything was going so well it was hard not to smile. I had a best friend who was amazingly awesome, supportive, fun, kind and liked me for me. I had a boyfriend - and yes, after the "L" word I had to admit that we were a couple and not just having a vacation fling - who I was head over heels for and who loved me back; who made me feel things I had never imagined possible and who had shown me what it meant to be desired. And thanks to Lex, for the second time in my life I had made a friend.

I still marveled that this had become my life. That in less than a month my entire existence had been turned upside down and inside out and I had come out on top.

I smiled to myself as I had a shower and got ready for the day. I was about to head downstairs when I realized I hadn't checked my scope yet. Surprised that I had almost forgotten I looked it up:

~ As one door closes another door invariably opens, so don't worry that you have been denied. The universe always presents us with alternatives ~

For a moment my smile faded. It had a positive outcome, but it foreshadowed something negative happening. I had just been thinking about how lucky I was to have Kass, Kail and Lex in my life. Did this mean I was about to lose one of them?

A cold dread filled my heart and I wanted to burst into tears. The idea of having any one of them out of my life felt like too much to bear.

I took a slow, deep breath and reminded myself that it could mean anything. I loved them all in their own ways and I believed they all loved me in their own ways. I didn't believe any one of them would leave me. Maybe it had something to do with the flight to Helena or my life there. Maybe my boss would call and fire me today and make my choice about the future easier.

I headed down to have breakfast with a smile on face once more as I reminded myself that I loved and was loved and no one could take that away.

It was a pretty low key, uneventful day. Kass and I had breakfast and I helped her with some scrabooking project for Lex's birthday.

After Kail got home we had a late lunch together and then played some Wii until Kass started making dinner.

As she cooked the two of us snuck upstairs to lay in each other's arms, look deep into each other's eyes and love each other like there was no tomorrow.

And we did just that, until we heard Liam's voice say awkwardly from the other side of the door, "My beloved wife asks if the two of you could kindly untangle yourselves from yourselves and join us for dinner."

We stifled our laughter until we'd heard him go down the stairs. Poor Liam, sometimes Kass's sense of humor must be hard for him to live with.

What Liam's awkward message failed to relay was the fact that Lex was joining us for dinner. She looked more, for lack of a better word, normal, than I had ever seen her before. She wore a pair of forest green leggings with a patchwork tunic designed to look like Sally from Nightmare Before Christmas. Shockingly, she wore no makeup and her hair was pulled back into a simple pony tail. When she turned to me I could see the smile on her face and the light in her eyes.

That look said it all. I knew that her and Dell were back together. It was impossible to see the look of pure, unadulterated joy on her face and not be happy for her.

We all ate as Lex gushed about Dell. She was so happy, excited and hopeful. Kass and Liam said all the right things, being supportive and encouraging; but they kept exchanging concerned glances. I didn't know Dell and I only knew snippets of their history together so it was easy for me to genuinely be supportive, encouraging and happy for her. Kail was mostly indifferent and excused himself from the table early, whispering in my ear, "I thought you two might need some time to talk," as he left.

After everyone had finished eating Lex did indeed drag me to Kass's craft room to talk.

"I feel bad that we just met and started to hang out and get to know each other and now I'm all wrapped up in things with Dell. I tend to get really wrapped up in relationships and all my friendships get put on the back burner, and you aren't here for much longer so I hope we can hang out a bit more before you go. I just want you to know you are an awesome person and I do consider you a friend and want to spend time together, but if I'm MIA it's not because of you. Is that okay?"

She looked concerned and anxious, I gave her a big hug to ease some of her worry, "It's totally okay! I completely understand and I am so happy for you!!!"

We sat and talked some more - actually Lex talked about Dell and I smiled and nodded - until her cell phone rang and she answered, "Hi baby! I've been thinking about you all day!"

I quietly left the room to give them some privacy and headed upstairs to check on Kail.

He was lying in bed in his boxers pouring over a textbook when I walked in. I climbed onto the bed and lay down with my head in his lap. We cuddled like that as he finished his chapter, then he bent down to kiss my forehead, "Is everything okay?" he asked softly.

I looked up at him and smiled, "Everything is okay. Lex said she's pretty wrapped up in her and Dell getting back together so we probably won't see each other much and I totally understand that. I mean, it would have been nice to be able to hang out and getting to know her a little more, but just because she's busy now doesn't mean we'll never talk again."

We laid there in silence just holding each other for a while until Kail kissed me, long, slowly and deeply. I was lost in his touch and his kiss as evening faded into night. Once again I fell asleep in his arms and knew happiness beyond measure.

NOVEMBER 22

I woke up slowly, the way you do when the whole world is perfectly still and you wake up of your own free will because you are completely rested. I smiled to myself and looked over at Kail.

He was already awake, propped up on his side and staring right at me.

That jolted me awake and I instinctively grasped the sheets around myself and pulled away.

"What's wrong?" he asked, confused and a little hurt as he reached his hand out towards me.

"Why are you just lying there staring at me?" I demanded, clutching the sheets to my chest even tighter.

"Because you are beautiful and adorable and I love you," he said with a tone of annoyance in his voice now.

"Well…that's sweet…but don't…its creepy!"

His face fell and he looked away. Now I felt bad. I reached out and stroked his cheek and kissed his forehead, "It's a sweet sentiment, and I love you too, but waking up to someone staring at you, no matter who it is or why they are doing it, is just downright creepy. Now I need to go shower and then start helping Kass prepare."

It took a moment, but I let the bed sheet fall away before I got up. Even though Kail had seen me naked more times than I could count, somehow in this moment it felt wrong to be naked in front of him, like I was more exposed than just my body.

As I stood up he reached out for my hand. I turned around to find him sitting on the bed holding my hand in his with his other hand behind his back, "This is for you. Happy Thanksgiving," he said as he pulled a card out from behind his back.

It was one of those turkey cards you make in preschool using your own hand as a stencil for the bird. Clearly he had made it himself and colored it using some of Kass's scrapbooking markers. The front said, "Happy Thanksgiving 2012" and the inside said, "Of all the things I am thankful for this year, the one thing I am most thankful for, is you"

I let out a breath I hadn't known I was holding and I felt one small tear fall down my face. I had never before felt so special or loved. No one had ever done anything like this for me before. It may have seemed small and silly to most people, Kass certainly would have laughed in Liam's face if he gave her anything like this, but to me it was the most precious gift I had ever received.

I squeezed his hand tightly as I bent to kiss him. With my lips pressed against his I whispered, "I am so thankful for you that there are no words," before I pulled away and said in as serious a voice as I could muster, "But there is no time for romance right now…there is a bird to stuff and cook and I can't let Kass do it all on her own!"

After a quick shower I checked my scope:

~ Today is a day for reflection and appreciation. Do not forget to share your appreciation for the special people in your life. They need to hear it ~

I smiled as I thought that for the first time in my life I had special people to appreciate, and they appreciated me. I turned to find Kail sitting on the bed staring at me as I stood naked next to his desk.

I put my hands on my hips, "And just what are you looking at mister?" I asked in mock seriousness

He got off the bed and walked towards me. I kept my hands on my hips and tried to keep the stern look on my face. He slipped his arms around my waist and said in a voice soft and deep with meaning, "I'm looking at the sexiest most beautiful woman in the world, who happens to be naked in my bedroom. I'm always afraid if I blink you'll disappear."

The sincerity and emotion in his voice caught me off guard and before my emotions could catch up, my logic spoke for me, "I do leave in two days."

He kissed my forehead, and whispered, "I know," then let out a slow breath, "That's why I'm trying to soak up as much of you as I can."

In that moment I felt two distinct and very separate reactions.

   1) My heart skipped and jumped and danced with joy that he felt so much for me

   2) Some invisible force with a pickaxe chipped away a little piece of my heart at the thought of leaving him

---

The day was spent in a whirlwind of cooking, cleaning and following Kass's orders. She changed her mind about the place settings at least four times and we seemed to be making enough food to celebrate Thanksgiving with the entire state of Texas.

Because Kass was a little over the top with the whole housewife thing, it wasn't just cooking and cleaning that had to be done. We also had to decorate. She had somehow found time in the past couple of weeks to make personalized place cards for the table as well as an elaborate centerpiece and garland for the chair backs.

By the time everything was cooked and decorated we had a full house. Kass, Liam, Kail, Lex, Dell and I sat down at the formal dining room table to enjoy the meal and give our thanks.

Kass had really outdone herself with turkey, ham, stuffing, mashed potatoes, roasted potatoes, yams, sweet potatoes, corn on the cob, three types of salad, homemade biscuits, cranberries, gravy and honey sauce. Not to mention the mountain of pies and tarts that awaited us for desert.

We each poured a glass of wine and as we dished up our food we went around the table saying what we were thankful for.

Kass: "I am thankful for my amazing, loving husband. For our life together. For my beautiful, vibrant sister-in-law who is also one of my best friends. To one of my other best friends, Melina, who has reminded me what it means to be a friend and who has brought me and my brother closer than we have ever been. I am so grateful to be able to share this holiday with all of you."

Liam: "I am thankful for my beautiful wife, my family, my career and my health."

Lex: "I am thankful for old friends," she looked at Kass, "And new," looking at me, "And my family," looking at Liam, "And having the love of my life back," looking at Dell.

Dell: "I am thankful to have found Lex again and to have been welcomed here for this holiday dinner."

Kail: "I am thankful for my sister and brother-in-law who continue to encourage and support me with school. I am thankful for the chance to really get to know my sister for the first time. I am thankful for my friends who are helping me follow my dreams. I am thankful for Melina, who has come here and shown me so much that I had been missing."

Then it was my turn. I felt like if I said what was in my heart I would burst into tears. Everyone else had stayed so composed and I knew I wouldn't be able to do that. I took a deep breath and jumped in, "I am thankful for Kass's friendship and constant offers to come and visit. I am thankful to Liam for sharing his wife and home with me so freely. I am thankful for Lex, who has given me her friendship so freely. I am thankful for Kail," I turned to look at him and the tears welled up in my eyes, "For everything," I said softly as the first tear fell and I fought to hold back the rest.

Kail took the hint and said, "Cheers!" as I struggled to regain my composure.

We took our time eating as we talked and laughed. We all shared stories of Thanksgivings past, about the events of the year and our hopes for the future. We talked about Christmas, which was almost upon us, and if people would be risking the Black Friday sales or not.

It was six hours later when all of the dinner and desert had been eaten, put away and everything cleaned. Lex and Dell had left and the four of us were sitting in the living room slowly digesting.

Liam was the first to declare the turkey had won and he was going to bed. Kass soon followed.

Kail and I sat on the couch cuddling in silence for a while. There was a comfortable closeness in our silence. Neither of us felt the need to fill it with empty meaningless words. We were both content to hold each other and share this time and space together.

Suddenly I felt as if I was falling and when I opened my eyes I realized that I had fallen asleep on the couch and Kail was carrying me up the stairs. I wrapped my arms around his neck and held on. When he gently laid me down on the bed and began pulling my clothes off I smiled dreamily up at him, "Go back to sleep, it's going to be a crazy day tomorrow," he said softly as he lay down beside me.

I curled up next to him and felt the fullness in my stomach from the meal. I also felt the fullness in my heart from all the love I had for these people who had welcomed me into their lives, embraced me, made a place for me in each of their hearts as I had made a place for each of them in mine.

NOVEMBER 23

I was rudely awakened by Kass banging on the bedroom door yelling, "Doors open in two hours. GET UP!"

Kail jumped out of bed and started pulling on pajama pants and a tshirt, "You better get up, she takes her Black Friday shopping very seriously and she will leave without you if you aren't downstairs by the time she's ready to go."

I was still half asleep and couldn't really process what was going on. Black Friday wasn't really a big deal in my family. We had always stayed inside to avoid any madness. Thankfully, Kail was on the ball and he brought me underwear, yoga pants and a tshirt.

As I stood up from the bed and pulled my pants up he handed me a brush and elastic for my hair. I glanced at the bedside clock. It was 2:30 in the morning. I glared at Kass through the door, then at Kail who seemed to be supporting this madness. I grabbed the elastic and, without brushing my hair, pulled it back into a messy bun. I would show my disapproval by being disheveled and grumpy.

Thankfully Kass had made coffee and had pre toasted and cream cheesed a bagel for me. I filled the biggest travel mug I could find and ate the bagel in the car as Kail read my scope to me from the front seat:

~ The depth of your feelings may be making you uncomfortable but there is no point pretending they do not exist. They will bounce back even stronger than before ~

After reading it he paused, then said, "Does this mean your grumpy right now because of a depth of feeling and you're pretending it doesn't exist?"

I slapped him in the shoulder as I reached for my phone, "My depth of feeling is annoyance at being awake at three in the freaking morning and I am not uncomfortable about expressing it. Now give me back my phone!"

Kass and Kail laughed as I sulked in the backseat. How anyone could have the energy or the chipperness to laugh at three in the morning was beyond me. I tried to nap in the car, but every time one of them caught me with my eyes closed they would turn on the radio as loud as possible. There would be no sleeping until we were back home. I silently begged the universe to send a meteor crashing down in the heart of Texas so I wouldn't have to endure the rest of this Black Friday madness.

Sadly, no meteors hit the earth that day.

It was twelve hours later when we got back to the house. I had survived as best I could by making them stop at every coffee vendor I saw. By noon I was so jacked up on caffeine I was running up and down the aisles of stores handing stuff to Kass as if it were an Olympic relay.

I have no idea how much money Kass spent that day, but every spare inch of her vehicle (including Kail's lap) was full of stuff. Clothes, electronics, appliances, decorations, jewelry, shoes…it was an endless sea of merchandise that made me dizzy. Kass kept complimenting herself on how much money she had saved. I kept biting my lip to not point out how much money she had spent.

Kail had bought nothing, though he had encouraged Kass in each of her purchases. As if he got some sort of shopping fix vicariously through her.

My lap was full of my one and only purchase of the day (aside from the copious amounts of coffee) which I had bought to commemorate my trip. It was a painting by a local artist of a field of bluebonnets - the state flower. It was sunrise, with the sky bright shades of yellow, orange and pink. The grass was vibrant green and the blue of the bonnets was like the fading night. So much light and darkness intertwined together. It wasn't just the bluebonnets that would remind me of this time in Texas. It was the boldness of the colors, the vibrancy of them, as if they were filled with more life than it should be possible to contain.

After we got home and unpacked the car, I headed up to my room to sleep. Somehow Kass and Kail were fine after just a few hours of sleep followed by the shopping marathon, but I was exhausted.

I was flying home tomorrow morning and I hadn't packed yet. I knew there was so much to do, but I needed sleep before I could tackle any of it.

Just as I collapsed onto the bed Kail came in and pulled me back up, "No sleep yet my dear. Now that Kass has all these new shiny things she wants to re-do all the bedrooms, so she asked that you crash in my room so she can wash these bedsheets."

He half led and half pulled me into his room. He stripped me down and laid me on the bed, tucked me in, kissed me on the forehead and whispered, "Sweet dreams. I love you," and by the time he had walked out of the room, I was asleep.

I woke up to the sounds of laughter and the smell of grilling meat. I stumbled out of bed, pulled on a pair of Kail's boxers and one of his t-shirts and followed my nose downstairs into the kitchen. Liam was grilling burgers on the patio while Kass and Kail prepared all the fixings and made homemade fries in Kass's new deep fryer.

"Well look who woke up just in time for dinner," Kass said as she one-arm-hugged me while her other hand lifted fries out of the bubbling oil. I backed away slowly, making both her and Kail laugh, "No faith!" she cried out.

The food was delicious and the atmosphere was so comfortable that I felt a pang in my chest when I remembered this would be my last dinner here. Once again I was struck with the realization that here amongst these people, some of whom I had only known for a couple weeks, I felt more of a sense of belonging, acceptance, love and family than I had ever felt before.

Everyone told stories about the day. Laughing at my moodiness and constant need for coffee. Mocking Kass's obsession with how much she 'saved' with each purchase. Teasing Kail about how he didn't spend a penny, but egged Kass on with every purchase. Liam laughing kind heartedly about how much Kass had 'saved' and spent as he squeezed her hand and smiled at her.

As we cleared the dishes I said, "I'm sorry to eat and run, but I need to get packing for tomorrow morning."

Kass and Kail smiled knowingly at each other and I raised an eyebrow in suspicion.

Kail noticed and then laughed. "What?" I demanded. He just laughed again and ran upstairs.

I followed behind and found him standing in front of my bedroom door. I reached past him to open the door and when I stepped inside I found the bed made with clean sheets and all of my things missing.

I ran into the walk-in closet and sure enough, all I found were empty hangers. However, there were three suitcases lined nicely against the wall of the closet.

Since all of my luggage had ended up back home I hadn't even thought about how I would get all of my new things back. Kass had fixed that problem for me.

While we had been out earlier today we had seen some fancy luggage sets. I had commented that one of them which had shades of the rainbow all blended together was especially pretty. I was guessing that after I had fallen asleep, Kass had gone back and bought the three piece set.

I turned to Kail with tears in my eyes, "She didn't," I said softly. He just nodded his head yes and smiled. I ran over to him and hugged him so tightly that I felt his shoulders shake. He kissed my forehead and said, "We picked them out, and of course Kass picked up some more clothes she thought you just had to have. We packed all your things except for an outfit to wear for travel tomorrow. While we've been up here Kass and Liam have left for the night. We have the house to ourselves for your last night here, with nothing left to pack. How would you like to spend your last night in Texas?"

I kissed him long and deep as I moved us slowly towards the bed. We peeled off our clothes and lay down on the clean sheets and held each other.

Most people would have made wild monkey love the last night they would be with their lover. We didn't.

It is true we were lying in bed naked together, but that wasn't because of sex. It was so we could be as close to each other as possible. Not even a thin layer of fabric between us. Our bodies were as close as we could possibly make them, just as our hearts were.

We laid there and held each other, whispered to each other in the growing darkness of the room. It was as if we speaking in normal voices would make the real world come crashing in on this little universe we had created.

We touched and talked for hours until I couldn't keep my eyes open. I kissed Kail long, slowly and softly. Then I told him I was ready to wake up from the dream. "What do you mean?" he asked as he ran his fingers through my hair.

"I still feel like this whole trip has been a dream and when I open my eyes in the morning I will be back in my little apartment in Helena all alone and none of this will have ever happened. But even if it is just a dream, it is a more beautiful dream than I could have ever imagined and I will be all the more lucky for having simply dreamt it," then I felt his lips on my forehead as I drifted off to sleep.

NOVEMBER 24

I had been on vacation too long. I had gotten used to waking up whenever I felt like it, and the alarm blaring next to my head offended me.

Sure, Kail's alarm had gone off, but that went off next to his head and it wasn't me who had to get up to it.

I hit the snooze and snuggled up next to Kail for a few more minutes. The last thing I wanted to do was get out of this bed.

After hitting snooze three more times, Kail finally insisted I get up. When I refused, he used the only weapon he had…he got out of bed himself, pulled on some boxers and a tshirt and went downstairs, leaving the obnoxiously bright light on.

Kass had made a delicious breakfast of pancakes, bacon, eggs, sausages and fruit. We all ate in awkward silence until we were about to explode. It was as if my leaving was a big white elephant in the room and everyone was afraid to point it out.

After the delicious, but strained, breakfast I headed upstairs to have my last shower in Texas.

Just as I had gotten the temperature right, Kail climbed in behind me, "I thought I would help scrub your back," he said softly before he reached for the shower puff and soap.

As with last night, other people would have made it sexual. I won't lie and say I wasn't insanely turned on by the whole thing, but that wasn't its purpose. It was closeness, intimacy, sensuality and tenderness that we sought amidst the steam and bubbles.

When we were both entirely clean and so wound up that a strong wind could have made us both explode, we got out of the shower and toweled each other off.

Kail sat on the edge of the bed wrapped in a towel and watched me get dressed. He watched me flit about the room making sure I had everything, and when I reached for a hairbrush he said softly, "May I?"

I nodded and he led me in silence to the bed. He knelt behind me and carefully, reverently, brushed my hair and then pulled it back into a thick braid.

No words were spoken because none were needed. We had both been so opposed to the notion of love, and yet somehow we had both fallen so deeply and so quickly that neither of us was prepared for it. Neither of us was prepared for me to leave either.

We had both known this day would come, but we had both worked hard not to think about it. Now the day was here and we were both trying so hard to squeeze as much as possible from each remaining moment.

After my hair was done he sat down behind me, holding me against his chest. We sat there in silence holding each other until Kass honked the car horn. We bolted into action. Kail threw on clothes while I reached for my phone, my final item to bring home. Before shoving it in my purse I checked my scope:

~ Today is a day of transition. It will not be easy, but that doesn't mean you should let people push you around. Stand up for your choices ~

I had no idea what this meant, but Kass was honking the horn again and there was no time to mull it over.

In my dreams of flying home Lex was always there and I had sat in the front seat with Kass. In reality, Lex was not there and I sat in the backseat beside Kail, squeezing each other's hands so tightly my fingertips were going numb, but I embraced the numbness and squeezed back as hard as I could.

We drove in silence.

We unpackaged me and my new luggage in silence.

We went through the airport, got my boarding pass and headed to security in silence.

When we could go no farther together, I took a deep breath and looked at Kass. She had tears in her eyes and it was only now that I realized she hadn't worn any makeup. Then I took in the whole sight of her. No makeup, hair tousled and pulled back into a hasty pony tail, yoga pants and a t-shirt from one of Liam's many golf competitions. If someone had asked me just five minutes ago if Kass would ever be seen in public in such a state I would have vehemently said no. But here she was looking more disheveled and casual than me for a change. I hugged her tightly. Saying goodbye to me with her real face on instead of the one she plastered on with makeup, hair products, jewelry, and designer clothes - this was the greatest goodbye gift she could have ever given me.

We hugged and hugged some more and neither of us said anything. I fought back tears and when I pulled away I could see that Kass had started to cry. I wiped one of her tears away and said, "Thank you isn't enough," she smiled and nodded and whispered, "I was just about to say the same thing," and then we were hugging again, this time both of us crying.

Finally I pulled away and said, "I'll come back again, soon, I promise!" she smiled, wiped her eyes and said, "You better!" in the best tough voice she could manage.

Then I turned to Kail and the tears started all over again. I couldn't speak, I could hardly breathe.

He came to me and enveloped me in his arms. He held me tight and let me cry.

When my tears started to slow down he kissed the top of my head and then put me at arm's length, "Meeting you, getting to know you, falling in love with you, it has all been the best thing that has ever happened to me. I want so many things right now, but they all have to wait a while longer. So for now, I want you to know that I love you, but you aren't bound to me. I want you to go back home and live your life. I will be here, loving you, but don't let that stop you from finding someone who can love you in person when I can't."

I nodded my head yes and fought back my tears, "I love you too, and all the same stuff you said," I whispered.

Over the intercoms they announced pre-boarding of my flight. I needed to get through security and find my gate. With the adrenaline pumping through my veins I found the courage to walk away.

After two flights and seven hours, I landed in Helena.

There were no friends or loved ones there to greet me. There were no signs and balloons welcoming me back. There were no hugs or tears or a sense that I was 'coming home' to anyone or anything.

I texted Kass, Kail and Lex to let them all know I had gotten back safely. I had thought that texting them all would make me seem closer to them; somehow it only made them seem farther away.

I caught a cab to my apartment and walked into the cold, stale place I called home.

The walls were white; the furniture was muted natural shades. There were no pictures, no mementos, nothing to show any personality or life. It was like a show home…without the show.

I called my parents to let them know I was back. My mother answered the phone, "Robinson residence."

"Hey mom, it's me. I just got back home, thought I'd call to let you know I made it back in one piece."

"Well that's good. You can come pick up your infernal luggage that has been taking up space in our garage since you left. I'm making chili; I know how much you love that so I suppose you can stay for dinner."

I hated chili. I have always hated chili, but my mother never paid much attention to what I liked or disliked, "Sure mom. Thanks. I'll be right over." She hung up without another word.

The brief conversation with my mother had not helped to make me feel 'at home' in the least, but they were all I had here, so I went.

I walked down to my parents and knocked on the door. My mother answered, looked me up and down and said, "What on earth have you done to your hair?"

I pushed past her to get out of the cold, "I got a haircut, it's not a big deal," I said casually as I took off my coat.

"And what on earth are you wearing!?" she demanded with shock and disapproval in her voice.

I had worn the black tights with the green sweater tunic. I was probably showing more cleavage than my mother had ever seen on me. I just smiled at her and walked into the living room. I bent down to hug my dad, who quickly hugged me back and then shooed me away with his hand so he could keep watching the news.

My home hadn't felt like home. My parents' home had never felt like home. The only place that had ever felt like home was Kass's and I already missed it so much I ached.

After setting the table, I silently sat and picked at the chili and biscuit without eating while my mother railed against me.

"Did you have fun avoiding real life? You know the rest of the world kept right on going without you around young lady. Who knows how many eligible young men got snatched up while you were away. I hope now that you're back from your misguided 'adventure' that you'll start seriously looking to settle down and be a responsible adult for a change. And what is with your hair and your clothes? You look like a hussy, I hope you know. God only knows what you got up to down there looking like that. I just hope you didn't bring any diseases back home with you or we'll never marry you off."

That was the last straw for me.

"Thank you for picking up my bags from the airport and keeping them here while I was away. Thank you for giving birth to me and seeing that I survived into adulthood. Thank you for reminding me about who and what really matters. Goodbye," I said through clenched teeth as I stood up and left the dining room.

I grabbed my luggage from the garage and dragged it down the sidewalk to my apartment.

As soon as the door closed behind me I collapsed into bed, burst into tears and texted Kass, "I am back here and miserable. This isn't home. It never was. I don't know how I ever thought I had a life here. Please don't tell Kail how miserable I am."

Then I cried myself to sleep, hugging my pillow as if it were a life jacket and would keep me from drowning in the sea of lonely bitterness that was my life here.

NOVEMBER 25

I woke up alone in a room that felt as impersonal as a hotel room. My hand moved across the pillow on the other side of the bed and my heart ached.

I had always slept in the middle of the bed, the whole thing was mine to move around, mess up and claim. In my short time with Kail I had gotten used to sleeping on only one side. Somehow it made my queen size bed feel massive and empty to wake up on one side and have the other side so empty and cold.

I forced myself out of bed and into the shower. I hadn't showered since I got home, I was trying to hold on to every last little bit of Texas that I could and showering would wash the last of it away.

I cried in the shower. It started as a single tear, but it quickly turned into great wracking sobs that tore through my lungs like fire. I felt such a huge sense of loss and pain. They say that you can't appreciate the light until you have lived in the dark. I always thought that was a misinterpretation. I can love peanut butter cookies without having ever eaten chocolate chip cookies. But I was realizing that you can convince yourself you don't need or want a thing when you've never had it…but once you've had it, you can never convince yourself that you don't need or want it.

I had always thought I was happy with my life, and in my own way I had been because I believed it was all I was capable of. Now I knew I had it in me to have so much more, and it made what I had here feel so hollow and meaningless. In the hopes of combating my growing despair with some inspiration, I checked my scope:

~ You need to adopt a more positive approach to life.
The person you need to love most is you ~

I made up my mind to make the best of things. Now I
knew what I was capable of, I would see if I was capable
of it here.

I unpacked my luggage and put on a pair of jeans and a
low cut tank top and headed out to get some coffee.

An hour later I was at Starbucks savoring the sensation of
the caffeine flowing through my veins as I flipped through
a travel magazine. Having successfully left once, I was
eager to do it again. That one trip, though it wasn't very
far, had somehow opened the whole world up to me and it
no longer seemed impossible to consider traveling to see
the pyramids in Egypt, the coliseum in Rome, Stonehenge
in England or the Great Wall of China.

As I sipped and flipped I felt a shadow fall over me. I
looked up into the bright green eyes of an exceptionally
handsome man. He was tall, easily 6'3" with a lean, but
muscular build. He had the hipster look going with a pair
of faded dark jeans and a blue and green plaid shirt with
the sleeves rolled up to show his strong arms. His hair was
an indefinable shade somewhere between blond and red
that changed with the light. He had a well put together, yet
somehow scruffy and casual look.

Then he smiled and he had these dimples that came out of
nowhere and caught my breath. His teeth were perfect and
white, his smile wide without being too big, and those
dimples…they drew me in and made my knees weak even
sitting down.

"Planning a trip?" he asked in a voice made for radio, deep and strong with a hint of laughter in every word.

"Not really, just browsing. I just got back from a trip, can't go on another one just yet," I said, my words coming out slightly breathy in the presence of this Adonis.

"Oh? Where'd you go?" he asked as he sat down in the chair across from me. I feel like I should be annoyed that he's just sat down at my table without being asked…but how can you be annoyed at someone so breathtaking?

"Nowhere fancy or exotic, just to Texas to visit a friend for a couple weeks."

He smiled again, "That's farther than I've ever traveled. I was born and raised here, never even left the city. I've always wanted to travel but have never done it. The idea of traveling by myself seems so lonely, and I've never had anyone to travel with. I'm Kevin by the way."

He stuck out his hand and I shook it as I tried to process what was happening.

Is he flirting with me? How has a man like this lived in Helena his whole life and I have never seen him? He can't be flirting with me, look at him; he should be flirting with movie stars and supermodels!

"I guess it could be lonely if you were going somewhere you didn't know anyone, but I was traveling to spend time with friends so it wasn't lonely at all, and I'm Melina," I said as I let go of his hand and tried to keep my heart from beating too fast.

"Must be nice to have friends who live places you can travel to. Maybe I'll have to try and make some friends of my own in Texas and we could meet there for coffee next time you visit," he said with that laughing voice and those dimples.

He was definitely flirting with me. I'd never been flirted with before. I didn't know the appropriate response.

Then I thought about Kail. How could I be sitting here flirting with a living wet dream when just over twenty-four hours ago I was telling Kail I loved him?

"Well as lovely as that sounds…I kind of have a sort of boyfriend in Texas," I said self-consciously. Kail and I had agreed we were both free to do whatever with whomever and neither of us was tied down. Yet the idea of being with anyone else just felt wrong to me.

His dimples fell, "Of course you do, I should have known," then the dimples came back, "But if you think you'd ever like to go for coffee and talk about traveling somewhere you don't have a kind of sort of boyfriend…give me a call," then he passed me his business card and walked away.

I watched him walk away, it was a nice view. Once he was out of my line of sight I shook my head, took a deep breath and stood up.

I had tried to be positive and live my life here, but so much of me was back in Texas. It was too soon, I just couldn't consider anyone but Kail right now.

I should have gone to pick up groceries and get settled back into my life here, but I just didn't have the energy. I ordered pizza for dinner and escaped into a book. I fell asleep in my massive and empty bed alone. I dreamed

about a man who looked like a Greek God come to life
and a man who looked like a slacker rocker and I couldn't
decide which one I wanted to travel to Australia to find
kangaroos with.

NOVEMBER 26

I was dreaming about a talking kangaroo giving me a lecture on following my bliss when the alarm went off.

I hit the snooze button and rolled to the side to snuggle…but there was no one there to snuggle with. I let out a deep sigh as I got out of bed and headed for the shower.

I went through the motions of getting ready for work: shower, hair, makeup, clothes and my scope:

~ You must not allow people to pile more work on your plate. You have nothing to feel guilty about, whatever they might say ~

I took a deep breath and knew it would be hard to stick to this one. I fully expected to show up at work and have my desk piled high with stuff people had put off until I got back. It was in my nature to do whatever it took to get the backlog cleared up as soon as possible. I don't get paid overtime, but almost every day I skip breaks, go in a bit early and stay and hour or two late. I had decided before I came back home that I was done with that mentality. I would work hard and well, but only so much as I was paid to do. My life could no longer be all about my work. Today's scope seemed to reinforce that way of thinking…but I was afraid of slipping back into my old habits.

I wrote the scope out on a post-it in the scribbler I always carried with me at work to jot down notes. I would not allow myself to forget or give in.

After wolfing down a bagel with cream cheese at the coffee shop, I headed to my office. I turned the corner to my desk and almost dropped my coffee. There were so many files stacked up on my desk I couldn't even see my monitor.

I spent the next hour putting the files into some sort of order as they had all been randomly shoved wherever people could find space. Once things were in order I turned on my computer and found myself drowning in over three hundred emails.

Another two hours passed as I went through the emails.

Three hours into my day I was able to finally start doing some work. I was on the second file when my boss came into my cubicle, "Welcome back Melina. As you can see there is plenty for you to catch up on. I'm surprised you haven't made more of a dent by now."

I turned to her and smiled as nicely as I could manage, "Good morning Sheena. I do see there is plenty to catch up on. I suspect it will take most of this week for me to get caught up on the three weeks' worth of work here; provided the other girls can handle all the new incoming requests."

I saw the annoyance flash across her face before she put her supervisor mask of false pleasantness back on, "Perhaps if you ate at your desk and stayed a little late you could finish it by the end of tomorrow?"

I smiled even brighter, "Of course I can. Would that be at my regular wage, or time and a half?"

This time it was more than just a flash of annoyance, it stayed on her face as she said, "I suppose I can ask Jenna and Cindy to take on a higher workload while you catch up for the next day or so," and then she walked away.

It had felt empowering to stand up for myself. I turned back to my work and dove in with a new vigor.

At the end of the day I had completed about a quarter of the backlog and headed home on time. I couldn't remember when I had last gone home on time.

The downside to leaving work on time was that I didn't have anywhere worthwhile to go. All I could do was go to my depressingly boring and empty apartment.

To kill some time I stopped at a bookstore and browsed for an hour or so, buying a book about a time travelling salesman.

I brought my new book to a nearby Italian restaurant. I killed two more hours by reading as I slowly ate my lasagna.

Finally I had run out of options and headed home.

Kass, Kail and Lex were all offline. Kail had sent me a quick email about hoping I was settling in okay and getting back into my routine and how he missed me, but that he would happily wait until I could visit again.

Kass had sent a quick email going on and on about some new charm Liam had bought her to commemorate her exceptional hostess skills while I had been there. She wished me well on my first day back at work and said she missed having me there to hang out with.

Lex had written nothing, though she wasn't one for emailing in general and was probably too busy getting her relationship with Dell back on track to think much about my being gone.

I replied to both Kail and Kass, trying to be as upbeat as possible. I wanted to tell them both how much I missed them, how depressingly pathetic my life here was, how I had stood up to my boss today and how much I wished I could have stayed there. Instead I prattled on about nothing and tried to seem as if being back here wasn't like dying a slow and painful death.

To kill some more time I had a hot bath and read some more. I finished the book and crawled into bed before ten.

If being back home with no friends, no boyfriend, no source of fun or enjoyment in my life had an upside, it was that I would be the most well rested person in the country.

NOVEMBER 27

I don't remember dreaming that night. I got nine solid hours of sleep and it felt as if my body and mind had completely shut down for that period of time.

I did feel very well rested and didn't even hit the snooze button when my alarm went off.

I was up and ready for work with almost an hour of time to kill thanks to my lack of snooze button hitting. I surfed the internet for a bit and then remembered to check my scope:

~ You are about to come up against an obstacle. Be strong and stand up for yourself. Don't hesitate to pursue your dreams ~

Considering I had missed the usual window for reviews while I was away, Sheena had scheduled mine for this afternoon. I couldn't help but feel that was what my scope was talking about. I had never pushed for anything in my reviews. Never a wage increase, promotion, more benefits or time off, nothing. I had come back home with a strong need for a work/life balance that I had never experienced and wasn't even sure how to go about achieving.

At this point, the 'dream' I was pursuing was getting back to Dallas. I had used up just over half of my savings for my last trip so I would need to save up enough to go again, as well as get more days off. Even though it was less than a month away, I wanted desperately to be able to spend Christmas with Kail and Kass. That's what I would push for, two weeks in December to go back.

Still no groceries in the house so breakfast and lunch were enjoyed at the cafe next my work. I managed to get through three quarters of the remaining backlog by the time 3pm rolled around and I headed to Sheena's office for my review.

We went through the usual process of my work the past six months, my excellent results, the lack of conflict with coworkers, the lack of sick days and the extra projects I had taken on.

"Well Melina, that pretty much sums it up. Seeing as how you've now been with us for twelve years, you will be earning an additional two vacation days effective December first. Also, you will be getting the standard two per cent wage increase. Considering it's almost four, why don't you just head home and call it a night?"

She glanced at the door and then turned to her monitor. I stayed seated and cleared my throat. She turned her attention back to me, "Was there something more?"

I took a deep breath and let it all out, "As you said, I have been with this company for twelve years now. I have never once asked for more than the minimum wage increase - which is only about twenty dollars more a paycheck before taxes. I have never once asked for an increase in my benefits or vacation day allowance. I haven't called in sick in over two years. I do more work than anyone else on the team. I am the only person who has stayed in this department for more than a year without advancement or quitting. I continually take on extra projects and exceed expectations. I have never once pursued advancement or sought out any form of compensation for all that I do, and none has been offered to me beyond the allotted minimum. Now I am asking," I took a breath to give her time to soak in everything I had just said.

"I know that Mr. Landry in Human Resources is looking for a new Personal Assistant. I know he has done interviews externally and internally without success. I would like to be put up for the promotion."

She sat there blinking at me with empty eyes, as if she hadn't heard me at all. After a moment she glanced at her computer, then back at me and said, "I am afraid that is not possible. The position has already been filled by Cindy, she starts on December first. I was going to announce it at the team meeting tomorrow."

Cindy had no office experience when she came to us three months ago. She spent half her day texting people and using her work computer for Facebook, and yet I knew she made more than me and now had gotten a promotion she was completely unqualified for. I took another deep breath and continued, "In that case, since I will be staying within the department I would ask that instead of a two per cent raise, I get ten. I think my twelve years of dedicated service more than shows that I deserve this. In addition I would ask for an additional five vacation days."

Again she gave me blank, blinking eyes, "Melina, you are a great employee, but you have already been granted the wage and vacation increases you are going to get. There is no room for bargaining in this."

This time I was the one giving blank eyes as I said calmly, "In that case, I quit. Effective immediately." I stood up and walked out.

I grabbed the few personal items I kept at my desk (a change of shoes and some spare change for the vending machine) and walked out with my head held high and a smile on my face so big I was sure I looked manic.

As soon as I got outside in the cold Montana air I called Kass.

"Hello? Mel?"

"Hey Kass. You will not believe what I just did. It was impulsive and possibly very foolish and not at all thought out or planned. But first I have a question," my words came out in an excited rush.

"Um…okay?" I could hear the confusion in her voice and it only made me smile wider.

"You had talked about the idea of me living there and working for Liam and all that jazz…how serious were you?"

There was no hesitation at all as she immediately and excitedly said, "Totally serious! One hundred percent serious!"

"Good" I said as I laughed at her excitement.

"Does this mean what I think it means!?" she asked as her smile practically vibrated though the phone.

"I just quit my job!"

Her squeal of excitement was heard by everyone on the street within a five foot radius of me.

That night Kass and I spent a few hours skyping while I was packing. She had already arranged movers to come pick up my things in just two more days and arranged a flight for me. I was wearing a pair of boxers and a tank top with my hair a mess covered in dust trying to pack up all my books when Kail walked into the kitchen behind Kass and saw me on the screen.

"What's going on ladies?" he asked sounding confused and suspicious.

"I'll give you two a moment," Kass said as she got up and left the room. Knowing her, she was just around the corner eavesdropping, but I couldn't blame her, this was exciting stuff.

"Sorry I look such a mess, but there's a good reason. Today I talked to my boss and asked for a promotion which was declined. Then I asked for an increase in my wage and vacation days, which was declined. Then I quit. In two days I'm moving in with you guys and I'm going to work for Liam!"

I had heard the saying that someone's jaw hit the floor. It always made me think of those old Wile-E-Coyote cartoons. I had always thought it was a useless expression since clearly no human being could literally do that. But in that moment Kail very much looked like wile-E-Coyote with his jaw hitting the floor.

"You're moving here? Two days?" he stuttered as I nodded my head yes.

"KASS!!!" he yelled. I saw her come back into view.

"Is this a joke? If this is a joke I will kill you in your sleep. Do not mess with me woman!"

She laughed. I laughed. She hugged him as we both assured him it was real and not a joke.

"I love you!" he said hugging Kass.

"I love you so much!" he said to me as he awkwardly tried to hug the laptop.

"I need to go clean up!" and he ran off screen.

I must have looked confused because Kass laughed and said, "Since you left he's sort of been an emo depressed mess and hasn't showered, done laundry, cleaned up anything or eaten much. His room is pretty disgusting."

We laughed and she kept giving me hints as I packed well into the night. We finally signed off around two in the morning and I crashed. Images of bluebonnets danced in my head as I drifted off to sleep.

NOVEMBER 28

I dreamed of Kail and the life we could have together. I dreamed of a day when Kass could be my best friend and my sister-in-law. I dreamt of a day when we could buy our own place and build a home together. I dreamed of a day when I could watch him accomplish his dreams with his company and be the proud wife of a successful entrepreneur.

I slept in until almost noon dreaming of all the possibilities that lay ahead of me. When I woke up I had a smile on my face for the first time since I had been back.

I jumped out of bed, eager to start my last full day in this city that held no joy for me.

I grabbed my laptop and found an email from Kail at three in the morning asking if it had been a dream or if I was really moving to Dallas at the end of the month. I found an email from Kass at eight that morning with a list of things the movers would take care of and what I needed to get done. Her organizational skills never ceased to amaze me, but I couldn't help but wonder when she found the time to get a solid eight hours sleep with all that she did.

Before I showered and headed out in search of coffee and breakfast I checked my scope:

~ You are a force to be reckoned with. You have big plans, plans that will soon turn into realities. Don't let anyone stand in your way ~

It could not have been more accurate! I knew I was on the right path finally and I was not going to let anyone or anything derail me. Not even my parents - who I knew I needed to see today and let know about my plan. I refused to let my mother sour this for me. The trip to Dallas was the best thing that had ever happened to me. I just knew in my bones that moving there would be a turning point for me and that it was what I needed to do. I would not let her take the joy of this away from me.

I spent the day packing, organizing and culling my things. It amazed me how much useless stuff I had accumulated during a lifetime of doing nothing. Clothes I hadn't worn in over ten years, kitchen tools and gadgets I had never even used, an abundance of bath products and candles that could have filled a five person hot tub.

By the time evening rolled around I was pretty much set. I had my new luggage packed again with things I would need for the first week and everything else was ready for the movers. I showered the dust and nostalgia off and headed to my parents' house.

It was seven on the dot when I got to the door. They would just be sitting down for dinner and I knew that my mother would find it the height of rudeness to have a caller during the dinner hour. Impulsively - and a little passive aggressively - I rang the front bell and waited.

She answered the door wearing a pale yellow dress with pink roses on it, along with a pearl necklace and her hair and makeup perfectly done. I couldn't help but chuckle at the absurdity of it all. She looked like an extra from a 1950's movie about the perfect housewife - but she was far from it. She tried so hard to be something that had fallen out of fashion over a decade ago and she had no idea how absurd she was.

"What are you doing here? You know it is our dinner hour, how dare you interrupt us! What are you laughing at!?" Her hands were on her hips and she even stopped her little foot at the last word, making me laugh out loud.

"I have some news mother, I figured since I knew you would both be in the same room for the next hour this was a good time to kill two birds with one stone," I said as I stepped around her into the house. I kicked off my boots and headed for the dining room.

My father was sitting at the table sneaking extra pork roast onto his plate as I walked in. He put his finger to his lips to assure my silence. Mother was forever worried that eating too much meat would give him a heart attack so she only ever let him have half a usual portion size, leaving him to sneak more when she wasn't looking.

I winked my silent agreement to this little facade and he smiled warmly at me.

I realized in that moment that I would actually miss my father a little bit. We had never been close, but he was a good man with a good heart who had always done the best he could for me, within the confines my mother set. The problem was that they were a package deal and I certainly would not miss my mother.

Mother came into the room in a cloud of Chanel No5 and silent hostility, "Better say what you need to say quickly and then leave so we can finish our dinner in peace, young lady," her hands were still on her hips - this was her disapproving pose - the same one she had used the time I dressed up as Charlie Chaplain instead of Marilyn Monroe for Halloween.

I took a deep breath and jumped right in, "I have quit my job and I am moving to Dallas. The movers arrive at my place tomorrow morning at ten and I fly out at two. I have brought my set of your house keys for you as well as a copy of my contact information for where you can reach me in Dallas. I already have a job lined up which I will start next Monday and I will be staying with friends until I have enough to get a place of my own. Thank you for bringing me into this world and for raising me the best way you knew how. Now it's time for me to finish the job on my own."

My mother's hands had fallen to her sides and she had her lips pursed tightly together as she held words inside. As our eyes met she opened her mouth and raised her hand to point a perfectly manicured finger at me, but my father cut her off, "Joan, leave her be. We have done our job; she is an adult and fully capable of making her own choices. Clearly this means a great deal to her and she has obviously put a lot of thought into this plan," then he turned to me and smiled, "You have our blessing dear, I hope you find everything you hope for there."

As I was about to thank him my mother exploded, "No! No! You will not do this to me!"

Before I could respond my father had banged his hand down on the table, making everything on it shake, "No Joan, you will not deprive her of this. You will give her your blessing and leave it alone. Remember your promise to me and do as I say!"

I had no idea what promise she had made, but to my shock and awe…she obeyed him. She sat down in her chair, folded her hands in her lap, took a deep breath and then looked into my eyes with tears at the edges of hers, "I give you my blessing," the words were said in a voice that was almost a whisper, but had a hard edge to it.

I nodded my head to her in acknowledgment, and then

turned to meet my father's gaze, "Thank you," I said softly. I turned and left before anyone could say anything more.

Back at my apartment I ordered in dinner, ate as I skyped with Kass about the final few things to do, and then I had a long hot bath. I ran over the visit to my parents in my head too many times to count. I was baffled by it, and knew I would probably never know what promise my mother had made, but couldn't help but wonder why my father had put up with her ordering him around all these years if he had the ability to stand up to her. I contemplated the compromises people make in relationships and swore to myself that I would never compromise my right to voice my thoughts and feelings or to do what I felt was right. Not for Kail, not for any one.

I fell asleep by eleven as I thought about the promises we make; to others and to ourselves.

NOVEMBER 29

I don't remember dreaming that night. It was one of those nights where you feel like as soon as your head hits the pillow that your alarm goes off and wakes you up again.

In my exhausted and grumpy state I wanted to hate the alarm. I pictured myself smashing it into a million tiny pieces as I hit the snooze button harder than necessary.

Then I remembered that the alarm was going off to give me time to shower and get dressed before the movers got here, and I jumped out of bed with a smile on my face.

I showered and threw on a pair of yoga pants and a tunic style knit sweater and headed out in search of coffee and bagels.

As I stood in line at the coffee shop I checked out my horoscope:

~ *Be prepared to turn your life upside down. Change is needed to bring success* ~

Once again it was bang on. Today was all about change in so many ways and I was so eager that it sent shivers down my spine.

It took four hours for the movers to clear out my apartment completely. I quickly give it a once over, wipe down and then knocked on the door of my building manager. We did a quick walk through and he cut me a cheque for my damage deposit refund and I was on my way.

The airport felt so dead compared to flying during the Thanksgiving rush. Everyone else seemed so mellow and too tired to care much about much. I felt so out of my place as I practically vibrated with excitement - and a fair bit of caffeine.

My logical mind told me I should sleep during the flight, but I was too excited to sleep. Every time I closed my eyes I saw images of Kail, Kass and Lex running through my mind and the thrill of being with them all again jolted through me like electricity.

The idea that the only place in my life which had ever felt like my imagined concept of 'home' would actually be my real home in just a few short hours made me feel like bursting with joy. I kept smiling and grinning like an idiot...even randomly giggling quietly to myself out of sheer happiness. I'm sure everyone on the flight thought I had taken some serious drugs before boarding the plane.

My connecting flight was delayed for two hours thanks to some sort of a malfunction, but I didn't even mind. I had waited thirty years for this; I would happily wait a couple more with a smile on my face to see it come true.

By the time I landed in Dallas it was almost dinner time. The original plan was for Kass to pick me up while Kail was in class, but considering the delay, Kail was able to be there too.

I went through the arrival doors to see the two of them standing together with smiles on their faces. Kass was holding a sign written on bright blue paper that read "Mel, Mel, you've been missed...come over here and give him a kiss!"

Kail stood beside her holding a stuffed jackalope (the fictitious folk animal of the region) and a balloon that said, "Welcome Home!" with a bunch of happy faces on it.

I smiled and waved and resisted the urge to drop my bags and run over to them and throw my arms around both of them. I did my best to walk calmly over and hugged Kass tightly.

I let her go after a minute and turned to Kail. He stood there looking down at me smiling, but not moving. His hands full of the balloon and jackalope. I gave him a moment before I said, "Aren't you going to put those things down and hug me?"

He smiled even bigger - which I hadn't thought possible - as he dropped the jackalope and let the balloon drift towards the ceiling and threw his arms around me, hugging me tightly and lifting me off the ground.

I laughed and hugged him back…and hugged him back…and hugged him back…and finally said, "If you don't put me down we can never go home."

He laughed and squeezed me harder before putting me back down on the ground and letting go.

Kass had been quick enough to catch the balloon before it wandered up into the rafters of the airport and we laughed as we hauled all my stuff out to the car.

The drive home consisted of Kail and I holding hands in the backseat while Kass and I talked about how the movers did and how the flights were. We got to the house and Kail brought my bags upstairs as I helped Kass get dinner ready. We all ate and Kass and I filled Liam in on how the talk with my boss and parents went and how the move went. I hadn't realized until after dinner that Kail hadn't said anything since I had landed. He had hugged me at the airport as if he would never let me go, and since then he had been holding my hand or otherwise touching me whenever he had the chance…but he had not said a single word.

As we cleared the table I thanked Kass and Liam for everything and said that Kail and I needed to catch up. He looked at me with a confused expression, but when I headed upstairs he followed me.

Out of habit I went to the room which had been mine during my visit, but none of my bags were there. I turned to Kail and he smiled at me and walked into his room.

I followed him inside and found my bags on one side of the closet, which he had emptied for me. I noticed that half the drawers in his dresser were empty and open a couple inches. I saw that he had cleared off space on every surface so there would be room for my things. It was clear that he had intended for us to share this room together.

It was sweet and thoughtful, and he looked so eager for approval. I walked over to him, put my hands on the sides of his face, looked into his deep blue eyes and said, "Thank you for coming into my life, for caring about me, for letting me care about you, for wanting to be with me, for doing this for me. I love you," and then before he could respond, I kissed him.

The kiss was all light tenderness. Our kiss was as fragile as both of our hearts were in that moment, and it was perfect in its fragility.

When he pulled away his eyes were full of things he wasn't saying and as he ran his fingers through my hair he let out a big sigh and said quietly, "I missed you so much. More than I thought possible. It still doesn't feel real that your back."

I kissed him again, this time full of all the passion and joy and intensity that I felt at being back in his arms. Within moments we were on the bed wrestling each other out of our clothes. We made love surrounded by the silent intensity of all the things we weren't saying, but we were both feeling.

As we lay there together, limbs entangled like a pretzel, hearts beating and breath coming fast as the endorphins of our lovemaking started to fade, Kail squeezed me hard, kissed my forehead and let out another big sigh.

I looked up into his eyes as my own grew heavy with the need for sleep, and I whispered, "I am real, this is real, never doubt that," and then I drifted off into a dream filled with glowing hearts bursting through people's chests and love that shimmered around people like a pink aura of cartoon bubble hearts.

NOVEMBER 30

I was dreaming about an incredibly cute kitten meowing rainbow bubbles to the tune of 'I Only Have Eyes For You' when Kail woke me with a kiss on my forehead.

My eyes fluttered and I mumbled incoherently about the cat. He laughed, kissed my forehead again and said, "You need coffee, you're not making any sense. I'll be right back," and then he dashed out of the room.

As the dream faded and reality set in, I reached to the nightstand and checked my scope on my phone:

~ You sought guidance and found it. You now have everything you need to live your life free of crutches. Follow your heart and find your happiness ~

I smiled to myself and felt the truth of these words. I had sought out my horoscope to help guide me. I relinquished myself to its whims, and it had brought me to these people and this place where I finally felt like I could be myself. I was here where I was meant to be and now I had the tools to move forward on my own.

Just as this realization dawned on me Kail came back in with a cup of coffee. He crawled into bed next to me and put his arm around me as he handed me the delicious hazelnut flavored nectar of the gods. I took a sip and moaned in pleasure; he had made it just the way I liked.

"Welcome to your first day as a permanent resident of Texas!" he said excitedly as he cheers'd my coffee with his own.

I smiled and pecked a kiss on his cheek, "Welcome to the first day of the rest of my life."

ABOUT THE AUTHOR

Mariya was born and mostly raised in Edmonton, Alberta, Canada (with a small stint in Nova Scotia). Her parents – like all people – made mistakes, but did the best they could to raise her right.

She turned into a flawed, damaged, broken adult with many lessons to learn and many paths to walk. After making plenty of mistakes and bad choices, she eventually weeded out the negative and toxic people in her life and was surrounded by genuinely loving, supportive and healthy relationships. In this environment she thrived and found the courage and inspiration to not only follow her dreams, but live them.

She still resides in Edmonton, now with a man who fills her heart with laughter and love and a cat who cuddles her when he's in the right mood.

25366864R00127

Made in the USA
Lexington, KY
23 August 2013